"The world seemed to change that night, as though we'd become different people."

"Yes, that's true. I no longer really know what to think about anything."

"Is that why you refuse to marry me?"

"I haven't actually refused. I just can't take it for granted the way you did. I don't like being given orders."

"That's not what I did."

"But it is. You just assumed I'd jump at the chance to marry you. How arrogant is that?" She gave a brief laugh. "I once looked up your name and found that Leonizio means 'lionlike.' That says it all about you. The lion rules the plains, and Leonizio thinks he can rule wherever he likes."

Briefly she wondered if she was wise to risk offending him, but his smile contained only wry amusement.

"Except for the lioness," he said. "She could stand up to him better than anyone else."

She nodded. "As long as he understands that."

Dear Reader,

Rome is one of my favourite Italian cities, and it's a pleasure to set a book there, especially when it plays its part in making the hero and heroine understand each other.

Sooner or later most people experience a stunning moment when they do something they were sure was impossible for them. That's how it is with Ellie, a respectable lawyer who has never before allowed passion to overcome her. She yields to a one-night stand with the handsome, sexy Italian Leonizio and then has to cope with an unexpected pregnancy. Determined to keep control of her life, she refuses to marry him.

But she accepts Leonizio's invitation to spend some time with him in Rome, where he lives. He's hoping to tempt her into marriage, but he also wants her to feel the magic of the enchanting city. He's more right than he knows. Although they love each other, neither is prepared to admit it. Beneath their passion is a battle of wills that each is determined to win. This comes to a head when he takes her to the fountain of Trevi and teases her into performing a ritual that legend says will make her agree to marriage. But she gets her own back, making the crowd laugh at him, letting him know that she's a woman to be reckoned with.

It's a vital lesson, and one that sets him on the right path to triumph as a lover.

Best wishes,

Lucy Gordon

Expecting the Fellani Heir

—

Lucy Gordon

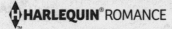

HARLEQUIN® ROMANCE

Recycling programs
for this product may
not exist in your area.

ISBN-13: 978-0-373-74391-9

Expecting the Fellani Heir

First North American Publication 2016

Printed in U.S.A.

www.Harlequin.com

Lucy Gordon cut her writing teeth on magazine journalism, interviewing many of the world's most interesting men. She's had many unusual experiences, which have often provided the background for her books. Once, while staying in Venice, she met a Venetian who proposed in two days and they've been married ever since. Naturally this has affected her writing, in which romantic Italian men tend to feature strongly. Two of her books have won a Romance Writers of America RITA® Award. You can visit her website at lucy-gordon.com.

Books by Lucy Gordon

Harlequin Romance

The Falcon Dynasty

Rescued by the Brooding Tycoon
Miss Prim and the Billionaire
Plain Jane in the Spotlight
Falling for the Rebel Falcon
The Final Falcon Says I Do

The Larkville Legacy

The Secret That Changed Everything

Diamonds are Forever

A Mistletoe Proposal
His Diamond Bride

Not Just a Convenient Marriage
Reunited with Her Italian Ex

Visit the Author Profile page
at Harlequin.com for more titles.

CHAPTER ONE

AFTERWARDS ELLIE ALWAYS remembered the day when things really started to happen, when the sky glowed, the universe trembled to its foundations and nothing was ever the same again.

It began gloomily, a cold February morning with the traffic in a jam, delaying her as she drove to work. Drumming her fingers against the steering wheel, she drew in sharp breaths of exasperation.

The world would call her a successful woman, a highly qualified lawyer employed by one of London's most notable legal practices. To be late for work should have been beneath her. But it was happening.

When she finally arrived, Rita, her young secretary, greeted her with agitation.

'The boss has been asking about you every minute.'

The boss was Alex Dallon, founder and head of Dallon Ltd. He was an efficient, demanding man, and it was no small achievement that Ellie had earned his favour.

'Is he annoyed because I'm late?' Ellie asked.

'A bit. Signor Fellani called to say he was coming in this morning and Mr Dallon doesn't have time to see him.'

'I wasn't aware that Signor Fellani had an appointment.'

'No, but you know him. He just announces he's coming.'

'And we all have to jump to it,' Ellie groaned.

'I wouldn't mind jumping for him,' Rita declared longingly. 'He's gorgeous!'

'That's not the point,' Ellie told her, severely but kindly. 'Looks aren't everything.'

'His are,' Rita sighed.

'No man's are,' Ellie said firmly.

Rita's response was a cynical look that Ellie understood. She knew exactly how she appeared to her secretary. Rita was a pretty, vivacious young woman with an eager interest in finding 'the one'. Ellie was a successful, efficient woman in her late thirties, with no husband or lover. Rita would clearly see that as a fate to avoid. To her, a man as attractive as Leonizio Fellani was not merely a client, but a dream to sigh over.

Ellie could understand how naïve Rita could fall for him. He was a man nobody could overlook, in his early thirties, with black hair and dark eyes that drew instant attention. He had a tall, athletic build and moved with a masculine grace that drew many eyes towards him. His face, she conceded, was handsome, although too often marred by tension.

Just once she had seen him smile, and there had been a glimpse of the kinder man he might have been. But it was over in a moment as the unyielding side of his nature took over again.

She herself ignored male attractions. There had been moments in her past when she had weakened, which was how she thought of it. But things hadn't worked out and she'd gathered her defences again.

Her appearance disappointed her. Her face was pleasant but not strikingly pretty. She possessed only one outstanding feature. Her hair. If she wore it long it could appear lush and wildly wavy. But she chose to scrape it back, tying the length into a bun at the back.

Businesslike, she often thought, regarding herself sadly in the mirror. *Nobody is going to sigh over those looks.*

She tended to judge herself severely. Many women would have envied her slender figure, but she considered herself too thin and overly angular. It was her nature to be realistic about her own lack of conventional attractions. Unlike Rita, she would never sigh over a handsome man like Signor Fellani.

He was an important client, wealthy, Italian, strong-minded. Curiosity had inspired Ellie to look up his name and she'd discovered that Leonizio meant 'lion-like'. It suited his commanding ways, she reckoned.

He had made a fortune manufacturing shoes. His luxurious, elegant products sold all over the world, especially in the UK. Just across the road from Ellie's office was a large store that sold them in great numbers.

His base was in Rome, but he employed this London firm to handle the divorce from his English wife. Alex Dallon liked Ellie to deal with this client often because her grandmother had been Italian and she had a basic knowledge of the language. Not that she ever needed to use it. Signor Fellani's command of English was like everything else about him: precise and efficient.

'Has there been any more mail from his wife's lawyers?' Ellie asked. 'The last I heard was that she was refusing to budge about custody of their baby.'

'But since she's left him and the child hasn't been born yet, she's bound to get custody,' Rita pointed out.

'I'm not looking forward to telling him that. Anything significant in the mail?'

'Not that I've seen so far, but I haven't opened them all yet. I'll check.'

She vanished and Ellie went to her desk. Taking

out the Fellani file, she glanced quickly through the papers, reminding herself of the details.

Three years earlier, Signor Fellani had made a whirlwind marriage with Harriet Barker, an Englishwoman he'd met while she was on holiday in his native city, Rome. But after the initial excitement died the marriage had suffered. When Harriet finally discovered that she was pregnant she had left him, coming back to England.

He'd followed her, insisting that she return to him, and, when she refused, he'd demanded joint custody of the unborn child. This she also refused.

Harriet must be a woman of great courage, Ellie thought. Leonizio was an autocrat, a man who demanded obedience and knew how to get it. In their few meetings he had treated her with cool courtesy, but she had always sensed an underlying steeliness. To the wife who was defying him he might be terrifying, but perhaps that was why she was so determined to escape him.

Rita appeared in the doorway, holding out a letter.

'He's going to create merry hell when he reads this,' she said.

Ellie read it with mounting dismay. It was from Harriet's lawyers.

Your client must understand that he has no rights over this child, because it is not his.

*His wife left him because she had found an-
other partner and become pregnant. Now
a DNA test has proved that the child she is
carrying is not her husband's.*

*She is anxious to conclude the divorce as
soon as possible so that she can marry the
child's father before the birth.*

*Please persuade Signor Fellani to see
sense.*

A copy of the paperwork for the DNA test was
enclosed. There was no doubt that the baby had
been fathered by the other man.

'Oh, heavens!' she sighed. 'What a dreadful
thing to have to tell him.'

'Especially today,' Rita said.

'Why, what's different about today?'

'It's Valentine's Day. The day for lovers, when
they celebrate the joy of their love.'

'Oh, no!' Ellie groaned. 'I'd forgotten the date.
You're right. But he's Italian. Perhaps they don't
celebrate Valentine's Day in Italy. I hope not because that would really rub it in.'

A noise from outside made her glance through
the window. She saw a taxi draw up, and Signor
Fellani get out. She went to wait for him in her
office, longing for this soon to be over.

A few moments later he appeared at her door,
his face stern and purposeful.

'I'm sorry to spring this meeting on you without warning,' he said, 'but something has happened that changes everything.'

Did that mean he already knew?

'I went to see Harriet yesterday evening,' he continued. 'I believed we could talk things over properly; find a way to make a future together for the sake of our child. But she wasn't there. She's gone, and not left an address. Why? Why pick this moment to run away from me?'

So he didn't know, Ellie realised, her heart sinking. The next few minutes were going to be terrible.

'She obviously doesn't feel able to talk,' she said. 'Perhaps you should just accept that it's over.'

'Over between her and me, but not between me and my child,' he retorted swiftly.

She hesitated, dismayed at the disaster that was heading their way. Sensing her unease, he spoke more quietly.

'You probably think I'm being unreasonable about this; pursuing a woman who doesn't want me. Why don't I just let her go? But it's not that simple. I can let *her* go, but not the baby. There's a connection there that nothing can break, and if she thinks she's going to make me a stranger to my own child, she's wrong. I'll never let that happen.'

Ellie wanted to cry out, to make him stop at all costs. Never before had this hard man revealed his feelings so frankly, and her heart ached at the thought of how she was about to hurt him.

'I need you to find her,' he said. 'Her lawyers won't tell me where she is but you can get it out of them.'

'I'm afraid it wouldn't help,' she said heavily.

'Of course it would help. They tell you, you tell me, and I go to see her and make her stop this nonsense.'

No! Ellie clenched her fists. 'It isn't nonsense. I'm sorry, I hate to tell you this, but I have to.'

'Tell me what?'

She took a deep breath and forced herself to say, 'The baby isn't yours.'

Silence. She wondered if he'd actually heard her.

'What did you say?' he asked at last.

'She's carrying another man's child. I only found out myself just now. It's all in this letter.'

She handed him the letter from his wife's lawyer, and tried to read his expression as he read it. But his face was blank. At last he gave a snort.

'So this is her latest trick. Does she think to fool me?'

'It's not a trick. She had a DNA test done and that proves it.'

'A DNA test? But surely they can't be done before the child is born? It's too dangerous.'

'That was true once. But recently new techniques have been developed, and it can be done safely while a baby is still in the womb.'

'But they'd have needed to compare the child's DNA with mine. I haven't given a sample so they can't have.'

'They got a sample from the other man in her life and compared it with that,' Ellie said. 'The result was positive. I'm afraid there's no doubt he's the father. You'll find it here.'

He took the paper she held out. Ellie tensed, waiting for the storm to break. This man couldn't tolerate being defied, and the discovery of his soon-to-be ex-wife's treachery would provoke an explosion of temper.

But nothing happened. A terrible stillness had descended on him as he stared at the message that meant devastation to all his hopes. The colour drained from his face, leaving it with a greyish pallor that might have belonged to a dead man.

At last he spoke in a toneless voice. 'Can I believe the test?'

'I know the lab that did it,' she said. 'They are completely reliable. I'm afraid it's true.'

Suddenly he turned away and slammed his fist down on the desk.

'Fool!' he raged. *'Fool!'*

Her temper rose. 'So you think I'm a fool for telling you what you don't want to know?'

'Not you,' he snapped. '*Me!* To be taken in by that woman and her cheap tricks—I must be the biggest fool in creation.'

Her anger faded. His self-blame took her by surprise.

His back was still turned to her, but the angle of the window caught his face. It was only a faint reflection, but she managed to see that he had closed his eyes.

He was more easily hurt than she'd suspected. And his way of coping was to retreat deep inside himself.

But perhaps a little sympathy could still reach him. Gently she touched his arm.

'I know this is hard for you,' she began.

'Nothing I can't cope with,' he said firmly, drawing away from her. 'It's time I was going. You know where I'm staying?'

'Yes.' She named the hotel.

'Send my bill there and I'll go as soon as it's paid. Sorry to have troubled you.'

He gave her a brief nod and departed, leaving her feeling snubbed. One brief expression of sympathy had been enough to make him flee her. But then, she reflected, he hadn't become a successful businessman by allowing people to get close.

For his wife he'd made an exception, and it had been a shattering mistake.

Ellie got back to work, setting out his bill then working out a response to the lawyer's letter. It took her a few minutes to write a conventional reply, but when she read it through she couldn't be satisfied. Something told her that Signor Fellani would dislike the restrained wording.

Yet is there any way to phrase this that wouldn't annoy him? she wondered. *He seems to spend his whole life on the verge of a furious temper. Still, I suppose I can hardly blame him now.*

She rephrased the letter and considered it critically.

I should have done this while he was here, she mused. *Then I could have got his agreement to it. Perhaps I'd better go and see him now, and get this settled.*

She went to find Rita.

'I have to leave. I need to talk to Signor Fellani again. My goodness! Look at the weather.'

'Snowing fit to bust,' Rita agreed, glancing out of the window. 'I don't envy you driving in that.'

'Nor do I. But it has to be done.'

She hurried outside to where her car was parked, and turned onto the route that led to the hotel. It was about a mile away, and the last hundred yards took her along the River Thames.

Driving slowly because of the snow, she glanced at the pavement, and tensed at what she saw.

He was there by the wall, staring out over the river. A pause in the traffic gave her time to study him as he stood, wrapped in some private world, oblivious to his surroundings, unaware of the snow engulfing him.

She found a space to park, then hurried across the road to Leonizio.

'*Signore!*' she called. 'I was on my way to your hotel. It's lucky I happened to notice you here.'

He regarded her, and she had a strange sensation that he didn't recognise her through the snow.

'It's me,' she said. 'Your lawyer. We have business to discuss. My car's waiting over there.'

'Then we'd better go before you catch your death of cold.'

'Or you catch yours,' she retorted. 'You're soaking.'

'Don't bother about me. Let's go.'

She led him across the road to where two cars were parked, one shabby, one new and clearly expensive. He headed for the shabby one.

'Not that one,' Ellie called, opening the door of the luxury vehicle. 'Over here.'

'This?' he demanded in disbelief. 'This is yours?'

Obviously he felt that the decrepit little wreck

was more her style, she thought, trying not to be offended.

'I like to own a nice car,' she said coolly. 'Get in.'

He did so, and sat in silence while she took the wheel and drove to the hotel. As she pulled into the car park he said, 'You're shivering. You got wet.'

'I'll be all right when I get home. But first I must come in and show you the letter I wrote to your wife's lawyer.'

The Handrin Hotel was famed for its luxury, and as she entered it she could understand why. The man who could afford to stay here was hugely successful.

They took the elevator up to his opulent suite on the top floor. Now she could see him more clearly and was even more dismayed by his condition.

'I'm not the only one who's wet,' she said. 'You were standing too long in that snow. Your hair's soaking. Better dry it at once, and change your clothes.'

'Giving me orders?' he asked wryly.

'Protecting your interests, which is what I'm employed to do. Now get going.'

He vanished, reappearing ten minutes later in dry clothes. He handed her a towel and with relief she undid her hair, letting it fall about her shoulders so that she could dry it. When he joined her on the sofa she handed him the bill, and the letter she planned to write to his wife's lawyer.

'I suppose I'll have to agree to it,' he said at last. 'It doesn't say what I really think, but it might be better not to say that too frankly.'

'You'd really like to commit murder, wouldn't you?' she said.

He regarded her with wry appreciation.

'A woman who understands me. You're perfectly right, but don't worry. I'm not going to do anything stupid. You won't have to defend me in court.'

His grin contained a rare glimpse of real humour which she gladly returned, enjoying the sensation of suddenly connecting with him in both thoughts and feelings.

'I'm glad,' she said. 'I'm not sure I'd be up to that task.'

'Oh, I think you'd be up to anything you set your mind to. Can I offer you a drink?'

Ellie knew she should refuse; she should get this meeting over and done with as quickly as possible. But she still had to get his agreement to send the letter. And she was freezing. A hot drink would be very welcome.

'I'd love a cup of tea, please.'

He called Room Service and placed an order.

While they waited she watched while he read through the papers again.

'How do you feel about the answer I planned to send to your wife's lawyer?' she said.

'It's a damned sight too polite. But you haven't sent it yet?'

'No. I thought we should talk first.'

'And what are you going to advise me to do?'

'Go ahead with the divorce as quickly as possible.'

'So that she can marry the father and make the child legitimate? Her lawyer said that in his letter, didn't he? And he told you to persuade me to 'see sense'.

'I wish he hadn't said that—'

'But that's how lawyers think,' he said bitterly. 'Let my treacherous wife have her way, no matter what it does to me. That's seeing sense, isn't it?'

'Don't be unfair. I don't see everything like that.'

'I think you do. After all, you're a lawyer.'

'Yours, not hers. If things were different we could try to make *her* see sense, but she's pregnant by another man and there's nothing to be done about it. The best advice I can offer you is to put her into the past and move on with your life.'

Before he could answer, the doorbell rang and he went to collect the delivery of tea and cakes.

He laid the tray on a table near the sofa, sat down beside her and poured tea for her.

'Thank you,' she said. 'I needed this.'

She sipped the hot tea, feeling better at once.

'How come you were standing by the river?' she asked. 'Did the taxi drop you there?'

'I didn't take a taxi. I walked all the way. And don't say it.'

'Say what?'

'*In this weather? Are you mad?* That's what you're thinking. It's written all over your face.'

'Then I don't need to say it. But you've had a terrible shock. You were bound to go a bit crazy.'

'Like I said before, I was a fool.'

'Don't blame yourself,' she said gently. 'You loved her—'

'Which makes me an even bigger fool,' he growled.

'Perhaps. But it's easy to believe someone if your heart longs to trust them.'

He looked at her with sudden curiosity. 'You talk as though you really know.'

She shrugged. 'I've had my share of relationship traumas.'

'Tell me,' he said quietly.

Her disastrous emotional life wasn't something she usually talked about, but with this man everything was different. The blow that had struck him down meant that he would understand her as nobody else understood. It was strange to realise that, but everything in the world was becoming different.

'Romance hasn't been a large part of my life,' she said.

'I guess your career comes first. Your car tells me that.'

It was true. The purchase of the glamorous vehicle had been one of her most delightful experiences.

'But there has been something, hasn't there?' he said. 'The path I'm treading is one you've travelled yourself.'

'Yes. There was a time when I thought things were going to be different. I allowed myself to have feelings for him and I thought he—well, it just didn't work out.'

'Didn't he love you?'

'I thought so. We seemed good together, but then he met this other woman—she was a great beauty. Long blonde hair, voluptuous figure—I didn't stand a chance.'

'And that was all he cared about? Looks?'

'So it seemed. Isn't that what all men care about?'

'Some. Not all.' He gave a brief cynical laugh. 'Some of us can see beyond looks to the person beneath: cold and self-centred or warm and kindly. Didn't this man see your warmer side? I can see it.'

'He didn't think it mattered, unless he could make use of it.'

She made a wry face. 'You said I'd travelled this road before you, and you were right. I don't normally talk about it, but at least now you know that this isn't just a lawyer "seeing sense". I really do have some idea of what you're going through. I know what it's like to be lied to, and to wonder afterwards how I could have been so naïve as not to see through it. But if you don't want to see through it—' She sighed.

'Yes,' he said heavily. 'If you don't want to face the truth, there's a great temptation to ignore it. You have to beware of that in business, and I suppose it's true of life as well.'

It was the last thing she had expected him to admit, but something about him had changed. He was speaking with a self-awareness that made him seem more pleasant. It was almost like talking to a different man, a kindly one who felt for her own pain as well as his own.

'I know this is all very hard for you,' she said.

He shrugged. 'I'll get through it.' But suddenly his voice changed, became weary. 'Oh, hell, who am I kidding? Can I call this managing? What she's done has destroyed the world. I wanted to be a father, to have someone who was really mine. My parents died when I was a child. I was adopted by an uncle and aunt who treated me properly but—well, we were never really close. I believed my wife and I were close, but that proved to be an illusion.

'Now I realise she was already sleeping with another man, but I never thought of it. Then, suddenly she was gone, demanding a divorce on the grounds that we were incompatible. I found out afterwards that she'd set spies on me to see if I had other women. But I hadn't. I'd been boringly faithful, which must really have disappointed her.'

'It certainly weakened her case,' Ellie agreed.

He gave a grunt of mirthless laughter.

'And she dumps this news on me on Valentine's Day. She could hardly have timed it more cynically.'

'Do you celebrate Valentine's Day in Italy?'

'A little. Not as much as you do in England, but enough to make me see the irony. The great day for lovers, except that it's smothered in snow, both physically and—well, there's more than one kind of snow.'

'Yes, it couldn't have worked out worse, could it?' she said sadly. 'I don't suppose she thought of that—'

'Of course not. She never thinks of anything except what suits her. But her pregnancy made it all different. The world changed. For the first time ever there was somebody who would be mine, connected to me in a way that nothing and nobody could deny. I told her that I couldn't let her go. She made a dash for it and came to England because she must have thought divorce would be easier, since we married over here.

'I followed her, determined to keep her, and if not her then at least my child. But now I learn that the baby's not even mine—'

'And I'm afraid it isn't,' Ellie murmured.

A tremor went through him. 'Then I have nothing.'

The way he said 'nothing' made her want to reach out to him.

'You think that now,' she said gently, 'but you'll come through it. There's always something else in life.'

'Only if you want something else. What I want is my child. Mine and only mine.'

He spoke like a man used to bending the world to his will. But there was a blank despair in his face, as though even he knew that he couldn't control this situation.

She guessed that such helplessness was alien to him, and he was finding it frustrating. He was used to giving orders, demanding total subservience, which was why this left him at a loss. Ironically, the strength he was used to wielding had undermined him now. She felt a surge of pity for him.

'There are other things to care about,' she urged. 'You'll find them.'

But he shook his head. 'Nothing,' he said softly. 'Nothing.'

She gingerly placed a comforting hand on his shoulder. 'What will you do now?' she asked.

He sighed.

'Accept reality in a way I've never had to before.' He frowned. 'I'm good at arranging things the way I want, or at least persuading myself that I've done so.' He made a wry face. 'Meet the biggest self-deceiver in the world.'

'No, you're strong. And you'll be strong now.'

'Why are you so sure? You don't know me.'

'Do you know yourself?'

'I guess not,' he sighed. 'Oh, heavens!'

He dropped his head into his hands. Touched, Ellie drew him closer, enfolding him in both arms, her instinct to offer comfort to him overwhelming. He raised his head so that their eyes met, hers gentle and tender, his full of confusion and despair.

'That must be how it seems now,' she said gently. 'But your life isn't over. You'll meet someone who'll love you and give you a child. And the two of you will be united in that child for ever.'

'You make it sound so easy,' he whispered.

'When the time comes it will be easy,' she promised.

'For other men perhaps. Not for me. I said I didn't know myself, but I do know a few things. I know I can come across as overbearing, so that even if I like a woman she recoils from me.'

His words caused a pain in her heart. Driven by an impulse she barely understood, she took his face in her hands.

'I'm not afraid of you,' she said softly. 'Life is treating you cruelly, not the other way around.'

'How do I stand up to life and fight it back? And if I win, how will I know?'

'You might never know. Sometimes the fight goes on for ever. But you don't give in. There's always something to fight for.'

A new look came into his eyes and he leaned forward until his mouth almost met hers.

'Yes, there's always something to fight for,' he whispered.

The soft touch of his lips sent a tremor through her, then another, with such power and intensity that she had no choice but to return the caress. And then again, responding helplessly to the sweet excitement of the feeling.

'Ellie,' he murmured.

'Yes—yes—'

She could not have explained what she was

saying 'yes' to. She only knew that the desire to continue doing this had taken possession of her.

She felt his arms going around her tentatively, as though leaving the next move up to her. She returned the embrace, moving her mouth softly against his.

'Yes,' she repeated. 'Yes.'

Then his arms became stronger, his embrace more desperate, and she felt herself drawn into a new world.

CHAPTER TWO

THE FLIGHT FROM London to Rome took two and a half hours. Ellie spent the time gazing out of the window, trying to escape the thoughts that haunted her. But in her heart she knew there was no escape.

She had thought of herself as sensible, controlled and disciplined. These were the characteristics that had enabled her to keep command of her life. Years of watching the aching unhappiness that had destroyed her parents' marriage had made her overcautious. Feelings were dangerous things to be kept to herself.

Yet Leonizio had destroyed her caution without even knowing he was doing it. He was a hard man, protected from the world. That was how she saw him, how he preferred to be seen. But suddenly there had been a crack in his armour, giving her a glimpse of the pain concealed within.

Even more surprising had been the sympathy he'd shown for her own troubles. It was the last thing she'd expected from him, and it had softened her heart, making her reach out to him even more intensely.

The result had been devastating. She had meant only to offer him comfort. Yet the touch of his lips had sent desire and emotion blazing through her, destroying common sense, destroying caution, destroying everything but the need to travel this road to the end.

Night after night the memories returned as she lay alone. The sudden cool air on her skin as he'd stripped away her clothes and laid his lips against her breasts; the fierce yearning for him to touch her more—then more—and more. Finally the great moment when he had taken her completely, and everything in her had rejoiced.

It was something she would never forget: the fierce pleasure, unlike anything she had ever known before, the blazing satisfaction as they both climaxed. The feeling of empty desolation as they'd parted, each avoiding the other's eyes.

When her mind cleared she was shocked at herself for having given in to her feelings without caution. But how could she have thought about it in advance when it had sprung on her out of nowhere, like a storm from a calamitous sky?

And if I'd seen it coming I wouldn't have let it happen, she mused. *Would that have been better?*

She found that a hard question to answer. Would it really have been better not to discover the fierce pleasure of his lovemaking?

And could she have turned away from Leonizio when everything in her had flamed with need of him?

When it was over there had been the dizzying sensation of seeing her own reflection, her locks cascading about her shoulders. It was like meeting another person and trying to believe that it was herself.

Silently she'd addressed the woman in the mirror.

I guess you're my other self. A different me, and yet the same me. I've never met you before, and I'm not sure I want you to hang around. You've already got me into trouble.

To make certain of it, she pulled her hair back again, fixing it tightly as before.

Now stay away, she told her other self, now fading into the mists.

If Leonizio noticed that she had changed selves he didn't mention it. He'd paid his bill and they bade each other a polite farewell.

He'd soon returned to Italy and after that they had communicated only formally. He had abandoned his claim on his wife's child and the divorce was moving to a speedy conclusion. That was the end, she told herself. Leonizio no longer needed her professional services and each could forget that the other existed,

Eight weeks had passed since she'd last seen him. She'd spent the intervening time telling herself that it had been a fantasy. Nothing had really happened.

But, with shattering impact, she had discovered that she was wrong. She'd been reckless to sleep with him, but they had used protection. Only it must have failed. It had to have failed. She was carrying his child.

To make her troubles worse, she desperately needed someone with whom she could share the news. But she was alone. Both her parents had died several years before, and there were no other family members that she was close enough to confide in.

Suddenly her life had become a desert. She was thirty-eight, and pregnant by a man four years younger than herself. Who else could she tell but her baby's father? However hard it would be to manage, they must have one more meeting so that she could reveal the news that changed the world.

By good luck some papers arrived that required his signature.

'Best not entrust these to the post,' she'd said to Dallon. 'I'll hand deliver them.'

'There's no need for you to go all the way to Italy to be a messenger,' he'd protested. 'There's a firm I can use to deliver this stuff.'

'I think it would help if I was with him when he signs, in case he raises any problems.'

'Fair enough.' He'd given her a friendly grin.

'You weren't planning on doing some sightseeing in Rome as well?'

'Well, it's my grandmother's city and I've always longed to see it.'

'Ah, I see. Get a sneaky holiday under the guise of duty. Very clever.'

He'd winked kindly. 'All right, I'll fall for it. You're due for a break.'

She'd smiled and let the matter go. Anything was better than having him suspect her real reason for going to Rome.

She'd emailed Leonizio that she would bring the papers and set off at once, without waiting for his reply. There was a flight due to leave that same day.

She landed in Rome in the evening, too late to go to his office, so she made for the Piazza Navona.

It was among the most prosperous places in the great city. Here, Leonizio's business centre was located, with his apartment two streets away. Checking into a nearby hotel, Ellie asked herself for the hundredth time whether she was doing the right thing in coming here. But these days most of her own actions confused her.

I was mad to come, she mused. *I should have sent someone else. I was also mad to go into his arms, but it all happened so fast I couldn't think.*

I have to see him. I have to tell him everything myself.

Briefly, she considered letting her hair hang loose, but all her defensive instincts rose against it for fear that he would get the wrong idea.

'I don't want him thinking that other me is still around. He must have no doubt who he's dealing with now.'

From their correspondence she knew his private address. As the light faded she slipped out of the hotel and made her way to the nearby street where he lived. There was an elegant block of apartments, with lights in almost every window. She looked up, wondering if she might see him.

Several minutes passed while she tried to pluck up the courage to ring the bell. But she couldn't manage it, and had almost decided to retreat when the sight of him at a window made her draw in a sharp breath. He pushed it open, leaning out, while she stood, tense and undecided. She was just beginning to back into the shadows when he looked down.

His face was in shadow but there was no mistaking the shock that pervaded his whole body.

'Ellie? *Ellie?*'

'Yes, it's me,' she called back.

'Wait there.'

He was with her in a moment, ushering her inside and towards the elevator, which took them up to the second floor. Once they were inside his apartment she walked ahead a few steps, then turned and saw him standing by the door, regarding her curiously.

'I couldn't believe it was really you down there,' he said.

He approached and put his hands on her shoulders.

'Let me look at you,' he said. 'It *is* you, isn't it?'

'Can you doubt it?'

'Maybe. You look like a woman I once knew— just for a short time.'

A very short time, she thought. *And we didn't know each other, except in one particular sense.*

Aloud, she said, 'Nobody stays the same for ever.'

'That's true. So tell me, has the divorce hit a new problem at the last minute?'

'No, you have nothing to worry about. Harriet has signed all the papers so far, and we've fixed a date for her to sign the rest. There are some more forms for you to sign, and then it will be pretty much over. I've brought a few of them with me.'

'Instead of just putting them in the mail? Thank you so much.'

'Things can get lost in the mail,' she said. She was prevaricating as the crucial moment neared, but she knew she must soon summon up her courage.

'Here they are,' she said, drawing out the papers.

He seized them eagerly. Watching his face, she saw it flooded with relief tinged by a hint of sadness.

'It's nearly over,' he murmured. 'I'll soon be free of her. But I'll also be free of the child who should have been mine, and that's a freedom I never wanted.'

'But soon you'll have the final documents, and then you can make a new life.'

'That's what I tell myself, but I keep thinking of that little boy. Even though he isn't born yet, I loved him so much. But the love must stop.'

'And now you think you have nobody to love,' she said gently.

'That's one way of putting it.'

'But it isn't true. I came to see you because—' She paused. Now that the moment had arrived she was suddenly nervous.

'I needed to see you,' she said slowly. 'There's something I have to tell you.' She took a deep breath. 'I'm pregnant.'

She wasn't sure what reaction she'd expected, but not the total silence that greeted her. At last he managed to speak in a voice so low that it was almost inaudible.

'What—did you say?'

'I'm pregnant. That night we were together— there was a consequence.'

He drew in a sharp breath. 'Are you telling me that—?'

'That I'm carrying your baby.'

'But we used protection. How can that be? You're sure? Quite certain?'

'I promise I'm not trying to trick you. You're the father. It has to be you because there's nobody else it could be. I don't know how but the condom must have become damaged. I swear I didn't plan this…'

'I wasn't accusing you of— I only meant—are you sure you're pregnant?'

'There's no doubt of it. I did a test. It was positive.'

Suddenly the tension drained from his face. Now there was only a blazing smile.

'Yes!' he cried. *'Yes!'*

He tightened his grip and drew her forward against him in a hug so fierce that she gasped.

'Sorry,' he said, loosening his clasp. 'I must be careful of you now.'

'It's all right,' she said. 'I'm not delicate.'

'Yes, you are. You're frail and vulnerable and I must do everything to look after you and our child.'

He led her to the sofa and nudged her gently until she sat down.

'How long have you been sure?' he asked.

'A couple of weeks.'

'And you waited this long to tell me?'

'I've been trying to get my head around it.'

'Is that all?' he asked quietly.

She felt she understood his true meaning and said, 'Look, I told you, you're the father. There are simply no other candidates. There's nobody else. You have to believe me.'

'I do believe you. You told me before that your relationships tended to be unsuccessful. It sounds like a lonely life.'

'Yes,' she said thoughtfully. 'It has been.'

'But not any more. When we're married you'll have me to care for you.'

'Wait!' She stopped him. 'Did you say "married"?'

'Of course. Why do you look so surprised? Did you think I wouldn't want to marry you?'

'To be honest, I never even considered it.'

'But you must have been thinking of the future when you came here to tell me. What did you expect would happen?'

'I thought you'd be pleased. You want a child. I can give you one.'

'And I can give you a lot—a good life with everything you want.'

'But I'd lose my career, which I enjoy. I'd lose my country. We barely know each other but you expect me to move into a new world with you—'

'And our child.'

'Our child will live with me in England. But I'll put your name on the birth certificate and you can see him or her whenever you like.'

It was sad to see how the eagerness drained from his face, replaced by something that might have been despair. He dropped his head into his hands, staying there for a long moment while she thought she saw a tremor go through him.

'It's too soon to make a decision,' he said at last.

Tact prevented her from pointing out that she'd already made her decision. Clearly he didn't regard it as final until it suited him.

'I'm going back to the hotel,' she said.

'I'll drive you.'

'No need. It's only a couple of streets away. Just a short walk.'

'But you must be careful about getting tired now. My car's just below.'

'Signor Fellani—'

'Don't you think you could call me Leonizio—under the circumstances?'

'Yes, I suppose so.'

'Let's go.'

He put his arm protectively around her. She gave in, letting him take her downstairs, into the car and back to the hotel, where he escorted her up to her room.

'I'll collect you tomorrow morning,' he said.

'We have a lot to talk about.' He grew tense suddenly. 'You will be here, won't you?'

'I've arranged to have several days off, so I don't have to dash back.'

'Fine. I'll collect you tomorrow morning.'

For a moment she thought he might kiss her, but something made him back off, bid her farewell with a nod and retreat down the corridor until he was out of sight. With any other man she would have felt that he'd fled for safety, but with Leonizio that was impossible.

Wasn't it?

After the traumatic events of the day it was good to be alone. She needed to think. Or perhaps just to feel. She went to bed early, hoping to sleep at once, but sleep wouldn't come.

She had a strange feeling of being transported back to the past, when she had been a child, watching the misery of her parents' life together. They had married only because Janet, her mother, was pregnant. Ellie recalled an atmosphere of hostility between two people who didn't belong together, even with a shared child.

'I should have known it could never work,' Janet had once told her bitterly. 'But our families were thrilled at the thought of a grandchild, and determined to make sure of it. So they pressured us into marriage.'

'Didn't you love Dad?' Ellie had once asked.

'I thought that sometimes there seemed to be love—'

'Oh, yes, sometimes. He was a handsome man and all the girls were wild for him. They envied me being his wife, but he only married me because he was backed into a corner. After a while I started to have feelings for him, and I thought I could make him return them. But it didn't work. Why should he bother to court me when he already had me there to do his bidding? You have to keep a man wanting, and if you can't do that he'll take advantage of it.'

Thinking back now, Ellie remembered that the only happiness had come from her grandmother, Lelia, who was Italian. She had married an Englishman, given up her country to live with him in England, and been left stranded by his death. When her son, Ellie's father, married she'd moved in with him and his wife.

Ellie had been close to her grandmother. Lelia had enjoyed nothing better than regaling her with tales of Italy, and teaching her some of the language. It had been a severe loss when she died.

Without her kindly presence Ellie's parents had grown more hostile to each other, until their inevitable divorce.

'Will you be all right on your own?' Ellie had ventured to ask her mother.

'I won't be on my own. I've got you.'

'But—you know what I mean.'

'You mean without a husband? I'll actually be better off without him. Better no man at all than the wrong man. Better no relationship than a bad one.'

Life was hard. Her father paid them as little as he could get away with, and Janet took a job with low wages. Determined to have a successful career, Ellie had buried herself in schoolwork, coming top of the class. In this she was encouraged by her mother, who told her time and again that independence was the surest road to freedom.

'Have your own career, your own life,' she'd urged. 'Never be completely dependent on a man.'

Ellie had heeded the lesson, took a law degree at university and qualified as a solicitor with flying colours. Alex Dallon was eager to employ her. She was a success.

The firm specialised in divorce cases. In the years she had worked there she'd witnessed every kind of break-up for every kind of reason. She'd soon realised that wretchedly unhappy marriages were more common than she'd thought. Men and women swore eternal love and fidelity, then turned on each other in a miasma of hate and mistrust. She wondered if love was ever successful.

Her own experiences gave her no cause for comfort. There were men attracted by her wit and her lively personality. But the attraction soon died when they were faced with an intelligence often sharper than their own, and an efficiency that tolerated no nonsense.

Finally there had been the man she'd described to Leonizio, briefly interested in her but then leaving her for a woman of more conventional charms.

Besides, how could Leonizio want marriage after the disaster that was his last one? His divorce wasn't even through. He'd be mad to even entertain the idea of getting involved again so soon.

No, whatever the solution was for her situation with Leonizio, it certainly wasn't marriage. They were both adults. She felt sure that they could come up with a solution for sharing their child that would suit them both.

Reassured that her sensible side had returned, she turned over and drifted off to sleep.

Next morning she went downstairs to eat breakfast in the restaurant. Her table was by the window, looking out on the street. After a while she saw a familiar figure appear, heading for the hotel entrance. She hurried out into the lobby, waving to Leonizio, and he followed her back into the restaurant.

'Did you sleep well?' he asked as they sipped coffee.

'Not really. Too much to mull over. You?'

'Same with me. Have you done any more thinking about what we discussed yesterday?'

'We agreed to be good parents, friendly for our child's sake.'

'That isn't what I meant. I proposed marriage. You were going to consider it.'

'I gave you my answer last night.'

He didn't reply at once, seeming sunk in thought. At last he said, 'We're still virtually strangers. It can't work like that. At least let's spend some time getting to know each other. You might find I'm not the monster you think me.'

'Or I might find you're worse,' she said in a teasing voice.

'I'll just have to take that risk. I want you to stay with me. You'll find the spare room very comfortable. My housekeeper will take care of you.'

'But—I'm not sure. It might be better if I stayed in the hotel.'

'The more time we spend together the better it will be.'

'But I don't think—'

She stopped as she saw a young man approaching their table. He handed Leonizio a piece of paper, saying, *'Ecco la ricevuta, signore.'*

Ellie frowned, recognising just one word. *Ricevuta* meant receipt.

'Receipt?' she asked when the man had gone.

'I've paid your bill here. I called them last night and paid over the phone. There's no reason why the cost should fall on you.'

It sounded fine and generous, but something about it made her uneasy.

'Last night?' she queried. 'Why? My bill won't need to be paid until I check out.'

'Actually—you already have.'

'*What?* You mean you—?'

'I told them you would be leaving this morning.'

'Oh, really? And the little matter of consulting me slipped your mind. So this is your way of showing me that you're not a monster?'

'I just want you to stay with me. Ellie, you're important to me—both of you. I couldn't let you go.'

'You mean you couldn't let me do what I want if it conflicts with what you want.'

'It'll help us get to know each other really well so that we can plan out a future that's good for all of us. Isn't that what we both want?'

Ellie regarded him with her head on one side. 'So that's how you do it.'

'Do what?'

'Conduct your business. Nobody else stands a chance, do they? You get the better of the other guy by doing something outrageous that he can't fight. Then you put on an innocent look and say, "Isn't that what we both want?" And he gives in. Or so you hope. And that way you get everyone so scared of you that they can't fight back.'

'Are you scared of me, Ellie? Strange that I never noticed. You're not afraid of anyone.'

'True. And in my own way I too can be fearsome. I keep my worst side hidden until it leaps out and catches you unprepared. So be very careful.'

'I'll bear your warning in mind. As for persuading you to stay with me—I guess I used the wrong method. Perhaps I should try another way.'

'Such as what?'

'I could beg you.' He assumed a slightly theatrical air. 'Please, Ellie, do this for me. *Please.* Stay with me for the next couple of days, at least until we can agree on the best way to move forward with this situation.'

Ellie had to concede that he had a point. They did need to sort things out. And maybe a venue more private than a busy hotel was a better place to plan their future. 'I will stay with you, but only for a few days. And I won't be sharing your bed.'

He nodded, giving her an unexpectedly warm smile.

'Whatever you want, Ellie. I only want to make this work. When you're ready we'll go up and collect your things.'

'Let's go,' she said.

Be realistic, she told herself. *He changed tactics and got his own way again. And he thinks he always will. But he's got another think coming.*

Upstairs, she packed quickly, then let him carry her bags down to the car. A few minutes and they had reached his home. As they approached the front door, a window opened high above them and a young woman looked out, smiling and waving down to them. Leonizio waved back.

The front door was already open as they approached. The young woman stood there, smiling.

'Mamma indisposta,' she said. *'Non puo venire oggi.'*

Ellie just managed to understand this as, 'Mamma is unwell. She can't come today.'

'Better speak English,' Leonizio said. 'Ellie, this is Corina. Her mother is my housekeeper.'

'But today she has a bad headache,' Corina said. 'So I came instead. I must go now, or my husband will be cross.' She smiled at Ellie. 'But first I show you your room.'

The room was large and luxurious, dominated by a double bed.

'The *signore* left before I arrived,' Corina said, 'but he left a note saying everything in this room was to be perfect for you.'

'How kind of him,' Ellie said politely.

So he'd left those instructions before she had agreed to come here, she thought. Just as he'd checked her out of the hotel without asking her. Those were his methods, and she would have to be always on her guard.

Corina helped her unpack, then went out to Leonizio, who paid her and showed her out.

'Let's have some coffee,' he said to Ellie.

He made good coffee, and they sat together in the kitchen.

'We can make our arrangements,' he said. 'You can tell me how you want things to be.'

'Is that meant to be a joke? How I want things? After the way you've controlled me today. You ordered the room to be fixed before I'd even agreed to come.' She gave a brief laugh. 'Suppose you hadn't been able to get me here? You'd have looked foolish in front of Corina.'

'It wouldn't have done my dignity any good,' he agreed. 'And you'd have enjoyed that. I'm going to have to beware of you.'

'As long as you realise that.'

Before he could reply the telephone rang. He answered it, spoke tersely in rapid-fire Italian and hung up.

'I've got to go to my office for a couple of hours. Why not come with me and let me show you around?'

'Thank you but there's no need. I won't escape. I promise.'

He made a wry face. 'I wasn't exactly thinking that—oh, hell, yes, I was.'

'I wonder what your employees would think if they saw how easily you get into a panic.'

'Only with you. You're the scariest person I know.'

'Then I'll just have to stick around for the pleasure of scaring you.'

He smiled suddenly, but his smile was quickly replaced by a frown. 'I have to be going. I'll be back as soon as I can.'

He departed quickly, leaving her to lean from the window, watching him until he vanished. She had a good view of the neighbourhood, with its expensive shops and elegant roads.

So many roads, she thought. And no way of seeing where they all led.

CHAPTER THREE

LEFT ALONE, ELLIE explored the luxurious apartment. Her own room was large with a double bed, extensive wardrobes and bulky drawers. Putting her things away, she couldn't help noticing how plain and dull they looked in these glamorous surroundings.

If I was in search of a rich husband I'd jump at his offer, she thought wryly. *But I'm looking for something else in a husband. Something Leonizio can't give me. Not that he'll ever understand that. He's got money and why should a wife ask for anything else? That's how he sees it.*

She switched on the television and sat watching a news channel, discovering that her understanding of Italian was better than she'd thought.

I could do with something to read, she mused after a couple of hours. *That looks like a newsagent just over the road. Let's see if they've got any English papers.*

Hurrying downstairs, she crossed the road to the shop, which turned out to be a delightful place, full of foreign publications. By the time she left she had an armful of papers.

But a shock awaited her when she arrived back at Leonizio's apartment. As she reached the front door she could hear him inside, shouting, 'Where are you? *Where are you?*'

There was something in his voice that hadn't been there before. It was no longer the cry of a bully demanding obedience, but the misery of a man in despair. She thought she could guess the reason. Once before he had gone home to find his wife vanished, taking with her the unborn child on which he pinned his hopes. Now he was re-living that moment, fearing that he was deserted again, seeing his world collapse and everything he valued snatched from him.

'Where are you?' came the frantic cry again.

Unable to bear it any longer, she opened the door. At the same moment he strode out so quickly that he collided with her, forcing her to cling to him to avoid falling. He tightened his grip and they stood for a moment, locked in each other's arms.

'So there you are,' he snapped.

'Yes, I'm here.'

'Come in,' he said, still holding onto her as he led her inside. His arms about her were tight, as though he feared to release her.

He saw her onto the sofa, then stood back and regarded her uneasily.

'Did I hurt you?' he growled.

'Not at all. But there was no need for you to get worked up. I just slipped out for a moment to buy a few things over the road. I'm here now.'

He sat down beside her.

'You should have left a note saying where you'd gone.' He spoke calmly but his face was tense.

'Yes, perhaps I should have done that,' she said, 'but I knew I'd only be away for a couple of minutes, and I thought I'd be back here before you returned. I'm sorry. I really am.'

She spoke gently, regretting the distress she'd caused him. When he didn't answer she reached out to put a hand on his shoulder.

'Finding the place empty made you think I'd deserted you, taking your baby, as Harriet did.'

His shoulders sagged. 'You're right,' he said heavily.

'But I promised to stay, and I'll keep that promise. So stop worrying, Leonizio. It's not going to happen again. If you need to go out, just go. I'll always be here when you get back. Word of honour.'

He turned, looking her in the eyes as though he couldn't quite believe what he heard.

'Really? You mean that?'

'When I give a promise I keep it. You have to trust me, Leonizio.'

'I do trust you. Completely.'

'But you're still afraid I might betray you as she did.'

'No. You're not like her.'

'Then relax.'

He smiled and squeezed her hand.

'Actually, I need to go out again for a little while,' he said. 'Why don't you rest, and when I return I'll take you out for dinner? We can start to get to know each other.'

'That would be lovely, Leonizio,' she said.

He seemed to relax but she knew the pain and fear she had heard in his voice had been real. It was there in his heart, and she would always remember it.

'Go out,' she said. 'And stop worrying.'

'I'll try.'

He departed, giving her a brief glance before he left.

She was glad to be alone again that afternoon. Since her arrival in Rome, everything that had happened had disconcerted her. Leonizio's reaction had only underlined how little she knew him.

But something else disturbed her even more. It was the memory of their collision in the corridor, the way his arms had enfolded her. She knew he'd been protecting her from a fall, but the sensation of being held against his body had been shattering, recalling another time.

That night still lived in her heart, her mind

and her senses. She, who had never before even considered a one-night stand, had gone willingly into this one, letting it tempt her as though it was the most natural and the most desirable thing in the world.

She had come to Rome because Leonizio had the right to know about his child, yet she was still determined to stay in control of herself and the situation. Perhaps it was going to be harder than she had thought, but she was strong. Whatever disagreements they might have, she would be the winner. On that she was determined.

She prepared for the evening ahead with a shower, followed by an inspection of her clothes. She had nothing glamorous, but a simple green dress gave her an air of quiet elegance.

She hesitated briefly over her hair, finally deciding to wear it pulled back, sending a silent message that tonight her controlled self was the one in command.

When she heard Leonizio's key in the lock she positioned herself so that he could see her as soon as he entered, and was rewarded by the look of relief that dawned in his eyes as soon as he saw her.

'Let's go,' he said.

His car was waiting below, with a smartly dressed chauffeur in attendance. He opened a rear door, bowing to Ellie.

'Take us to the Venere,' Leonizio told him.

Ellie gave him a quick startled glance.

'Is that the Venere Hotel, near the Colosseum?' she asked.

'Yes. It's got a fine restaurant. You know it?'

'I've heard of it,' she said.

Lelia, her Italian grandmother, had worked in the Venere and had described it as one of the most luxurious places in Rome. It would be fascinating to see it now, Ellie thought.

She understood its reputation as soon as they arrived. The building looked as though it had once been a palace. Inside, a waiter greeted them and led them to a table by the window, from which she could see the Colosseum, the huge amphitheatre built nearly two thousand years ago.

'It's eerie,' she mused. 'Once people crowded there for the pleasure of seeing victims fed to the lions. Now the tourists go because it's beautiful and fascinating. And maybe we've all got somebody we'd like to see fed to the lions.'

'You wouldn't be aiming that at me, would you?' he queried.

'I'm not sure,' she said. 'I'll let you know when I've decided.'

'Well, I can't say I haven't been warned.'

'Right. I can be a real pain in the neck. You'll probably be glad to be rid of me.'

'Forget it. There's no way you'll escape.'

She gave him a teasing smile. 'Surely you don't want a woman who's a pestiferous nuisance?'

He returned the smile. 'I might. They can often be the most fun.'

He held out his hand and she shook it. 'As long as we understand each other,' she said.

'Perhaps we always did.'

'No, I don't think we ever did.'

While he was considering this a waiter approached with a menu, which he gave to Ellie.

'Need any help?' Leonizio asked.

'I can manage the Italian but I'll need you to explain the food to me. What's *Coda all Vaccinara?*'

'Stewed oxtail in tomato sauce,' Leonizio told her.

'It sounds nice. I'd like to have some.'

'May I suggest the Frascati wine to go with it, *signorina*?' the waiter said.

'No,' Leonizio said at once. 'Sparkling water for the lady. No alcohol.'

'And for you, *signore*?'

'I'll have the Frascati.'

When the waiter had retired, Leonizio said, 'I know you can't drink wine while you're pregnant.'

She didn't reply and after a moment he demanded, 'Why are you glaring at me?'

'I'm not.'

'Yes, you are. You'd like to thump me.'

'That's very perceptive of you. All right, the way you made that decision without consulting me makes me think a good thump might be satisfying.'

'You do me an injustice. I paid you the compliment of assuming that you would already have made the sensible decision. You're such an efficient, businesslike person that—'

'All right, all right. You can stop there. You always know what to say, don't you?'

He gave her a cheerful grin. 'Luckily for me, yes. With some combatants it's a useful skill.'

'Is that what we are? Combatants?'

'Not all the time. But it's something that's going to crop up now and then.'

'Now and then. I suppose that's true.'

'And while we can have an evening out like this, we can relax together and find a way to solve the problem.'

His tone was friendly, but a man working at a business arrangement might have spoken in just this way, she thought.

'How are you feeling now?' he asked.

'Fine. That rest did me good. Now I'm in the mood to enjoy myself.'

'You're all right after what I put you through?'

'You mean when you got so upset because I wasn't there? I'm sorry for the whole thing. It must have been terrible for you, feeling like you were reliving the past.'

He nodded. 'It was exactly the same. I came home one day and she'd gone. She didn't leave a note. I was left to wonder until an email arrived the next day.

'Yes. Coming back to an empty house is something I don't cope with very well.' He gave a brief self-mocking laugh. 'I remember telling you that we should discover things about each other. Well, that's something you've discovered. Perhaps you should take warning.'

'I've already had plenty to warn me, and there's nothing I can't cope with. Beware. This lioness has claws.'

'Well, I know that. They left a few scratches on me when we were together.'

She drew a sharp breath. His words brought back the memory of the time she had spent in his arms, overcome by a physical excitement she'd never known before. Bereft of all self-control, she had clutched him in a fever of desire that it shocked her to remember now.

'I'm sorry,' she said hastily. 'I didn't mean to hurt you.'

'Don't apologise. It was an accident. The world seemed to change that night, as though we'd become different people.'

'Yes, that's true. I no longer really know what to think about anything.'

'Is that why you refuse to marry me?'

'I haven't actually refused. I just can't take it for granted, the way you did. I don't like being given orders.'

'That's not what I did.'

'But it is. You just assumed I'd jump at the chance to marry you. How arrogant is that?'

She gave a brief laugh. 'I once looked up your name and found that Leonizio means 'lion-like'. That says it all about you. The lion rules the plains, and Leonizio thinks he can rule wherever he likes.'

Briefly she wondered if she was wise to risk offending him, but his smile contained only wry amusement.

'Except for the lioness,' he said. 'She could stand up to him better than anyone else.'

She nodded. 'As long as he understands that.'

'He understands completely. And he knows he'll have to be cleverer than usual to achieve victory.'

'But he doesn't really doubt that he'll be the winner, does he?'

'Tact prevents me answering that.' He raised his glass. 'Here's to victory—for both of us.'

She raised her own glass and they clinked.

'As long as we each understand what victory

means,' he said. 'You know what it means to me but—' He paused.

'You just can't understand why I don't jump at the chance to marry you, can you?' she said.

'I'm not the conceited oaf that makes me sound. As a person I may not be likeable. I understand that.'

'Is that what your wife said?'

'She said plenty about me. None of it good, in the end.'

'In my experience, marriage ends badly. My parents divorced. You're about to be divorced. It's par for the course, it seems. Can you blame me for refusing you?'

'Yes, but don't forget that not all marriages need end that way. Ours would be different. We would be entering it with our eyes wide open. What do I have to offer to persuade you?'

'You don't understand. It's what I'd lose. My country, my career, my freedom, my independence. I'm not ready to rush into it.'

'Not even to benefit our child?'

'But does marriage always benefit the child?' she asked. 'My parents were married and the unhappiness filled the air. I need to know—this is going to sound crazy to you—but I need to know that we can be friends.'

'I don't think it's crazy at all. It makes sense.' He gave a contented nod. 'We've got a while to get to know each other, and hopefully like each other.'

'Yes,' she said eagerly. 'That's the luckiest thing that can happen to a child, that its parents can be best friends.'

'You think that's luckier than if the parents love each other?'

'It can be. Friendship doesn't have so many ups and downs, so many dramas and crises. I can remember coming home from school wondering if my parents were speaking to each other today. When I got the lead in the school play they each came to a different performance. It would have been lovely if they'd come together and we'd had an evening as a happy family, but—' she shrugged '—that's how it was.'

Suddenly they were surrounded by applause. A man had appeared, bearing a guitar. He bowed to the guests at the tables who were applauding his entrance, and began to sing. Ellie listened with pleasure as he made his way between the tables, coming close until she could see him clearly. Noticing that she was delighted, Leonizio signalled to the man. He approached them, carolling cheerfully, until Leonizio held out a generous tip. He bowed and departed. When he finished his performance she clapped eagerly.

'That was lovely,' she said. 'It's such a nice, cheeky song.'

'You understood it?' Leonizio asked, astonished. 'But he was singing in Roman dialect. I know you understand some Italian, but dialect?'

'My grandmother used to sing it to me when I was a little girl. She came from Rome; she was born and spent her early years in Trastevere and she told me so much about it that I longed to see it. I loved my grandmother so much. I used to call her Nonna when I knew that was what Italians called their grandmothers. Now I'm here I feel wonderfully close to her.'

'Tell me about her.'

'She's the reason I'd heard of the Venere. Years ago she worked here as a chambermaid.'

'Here? In this very building?'

'Yes. Then she met an Englishman who was a guest, and they fell in love. He took her back to England with him. They married and had a son, my father. Sadly, my grandfather didn't live very long. Nonna mostly brought up my father on her own. When he married my mother she lived with them, looking after me.

'So you're nearly as much Italian as English?'

'In some ways. My mother didn't really like my grandmother very much. She said Nonna was a bad influence on me. She was very cross one day when she found her playing me some music. It was opera and my mother said it was way above my head.'

'And was it?'

'No, I like opera because of its terrific tunes. That's all.'

'So if I want to take you to an opera that would be a mark in my favour?'

'It would be lovely.'

'You're so knowledgeable that I'm sure you know about the Caracalla Baths.'

'They were a kind of spa built by the Emperor Caracalla nearly two thousand years ago. There's very little left standing, but what's left is used as a theatre for open-air performances.'

'Right. They open every summer, but this year they're doing a special run in April. We'll get the programme and you can take your pick.'

'That's lovely. Oh, how I wish I had Nonna here now so that she could see me becoming her real granddaughter after all this time. She died many years ago, and I miss her so much.'

'You're going to enjoy Rome, I promise you.'

Of course he wanted her to enjoy Rome, because it would make it easier for him to persuade her to stay and marry him. A slightly cynical voice whispered this in her mind, but she refused to let it worry her. Leonizio was handsome and attentive and part of her simply wanted to relax and be with him.

A sudden loud noise announced the arrival of a crowd. The waiter dashed around, trying to find room for them all. Ellie closed her eyes, trying to shut out the commotion. These days she tired easily.

'Perhaps we should go,' Leonizio said wryly, looking at her. 'It's time you were getting some rest.'

'Giving me orders again?'

'Yes.' He said it with a smile that made the word humorous.

'In that case I'd better obey,' she chuckled.

A few minutes' drive brought them home. He saw her to her bedroom door.

'Is there anything I can do for you?'

'No, thank you. I have all I need.'

'Go to bed, then.'

For a moment he seemed on the verge of kissing her, but he only opened the door and indicated for her to go in.

'Goodnight,' he said softly. 'Sleep well.'

'And you.'

She slipped inside and closed the door.

Now she could go to bed and try to come to terms with everything that was happening to her. It was hard because so many things in her mind seemed to direct her two ways. Some were troublesome, others suggested the hope of happiness if only she could understand many ideas. Still trying to get clear, she faded into sleep.

Suddenly she found herself in a new place, one

where there were no boundaries, no definite positions. Here there was only mist and sensation, leading her forward into an unknown world.

But she realised that it wasn't completely unknown. She had been here once before in another life, another universe, one that was still offering intriguing possibilities. She could feel again the sweetness that had tempted her, the touch so different from anything she had known.

But there was also the apprehension at the way she was losing control. Deep inside her a nervous voice was crying out.

'What am I doing? Do I dare do this? Am I just a little mad? Or am I turning into somebody else—somebody I don't know? I mustn't do this… not now—not this time—'

Even as she spoke, she gasped with the tremor of remembered sensation that possessed her.

Be strong, whispered the warning voice. *Stay in control. You lost control that time and you're paying for it. You know that.*

'Yes, I do. And I mustn't—*no*—*no*!'

Then everything changed. There was a pounding on her door. The next moment Leonizio was there, leaning over her, taking her in his arms.

'Ellie,' he said hoarsely. 'Ellie! Wake up!'

The sound of his voice startled her awake. Gradually her breathing slowed and the world came back into focus. She found that she was clinging to him.

'Wake up,' he said again.

'It's all right… I'm awake now.'

'You must have had a nightmare.'

Her mind and senses were spinning. 'A nightmare—yes—no—I'm not sure—'

'You sounded as though you were suffering something terrible. I could hear you right out in the corridor, and I just had to come in and see if I could help.'

'Thank you but I'm all right. It was just a dream.'

The sight of this room was bringing reality back, but the dream was still there. It would always be there, she realised. As long as she lived.

His arms were around her and she could feel his hands stroking her hair, which flowed loose again. It was a sweet sensation and she yielded to the temptation to rest her head on his shoulder, enjoying the soft caresses.

But suddenly the pleasure stopped. He snatched back his hands and rose from the bed. He turned away to the door, but there he stopped, standing with his back to her. She waited for him to turn around but something seemed to be constraining him.

'What is it?' she asked. 'What's wrong?'

'When you were asleep you were crying out, No—no. Why was that?'

'I can't remember,' she said evasively.

'Tell me the truth, Ellie. That time we spent together—' a shudder went through him '—I've always thought you enjoyed it as much as I did.'

'I did. It was beautiful.'

'Yes, it was. I can remember when you were in my arms—feeling that I wanted you more than I've ever wanted any—' He paused, full of tension and self-doubt.

'I felt like that too,' she assured him.

He turned back and came closer, though still keeping a slight distance between them.

'But just now,' he said uneasily, 'I heard you crying, *No—no*!'

'I didn't say no that day. If I had you'd have stopped.' She reached up to take his hands, drawing him down to sit on the bed. 'You would have stopped,' she repeated gently. 'You're a good man. Much kinder than you like people to know. But *I* know.'

'I would never have done anything against your will, I swear it. But hearing you cry out tonight scared me—made me wonder—'

'Don't. There's no need to wonder. It was all lovely.'

'Truly? You embraced me of your own free will?'

'Absolutely. I wanted you. Couldn't you feel that?'

'Yes. At the time it felt so wonderful to be together.'

'At the time? But not afterwards?'

'Afterwards you seemed to turn against me. You couldn't get away from me fast enough.'

'That's not how I—' She sighed. 'I guess we misunderstood each other.'

'There's a lot about that day that I didn't understand, but things look different now. I wanted you then and now I want you for always.'

But did he want her, or only the child she carried? If only that thought would go away and leave her in peace.

'I guess we have lots to talk about,' she said. 'You speak of marriage but you know nothing about me except that I'm pregnant.'

'What else do I need to know?'

'I'm thirty-eight.'

'Why should that matter?'

'It makes me four years older than you, and it gives me a slightly greater chance of miscarrying. You might simply find yourself stuck with an older wife who can't give you a child. I could be very bad news for you.'

'Stop it, Ellie. Stop trying to put me off. I want you, and I want you to want me.'

'It's not that simple.'

'Then we'll make it simple.'

'How?'

'Like this,' he said, taking her into his arms.

The kiss he gave her wasn't passionate but gentle and comforting, filling her with happiness.

'We belong together,' he said. 'And one day you'll see that.'

'Perhaps,' she whispered.

'There's no perhaps about it. You're mine.' His words might sound demanding, but his tone was gentle.

'So I'm yours,' she said. 'That's an order, is it?'

He rose and went to the door, pausing to look back at her.

'It could be.' He smiled. 'But I guess I'll have to be patient.'

Then he departed, leaving her full of confusion.

She closed her eyes, trying to make sense of the crowd of impressions and memories that converged on her. But it was impossible. She needed more time to come to terms with Leonizio. The authoritative man she had known at first had seduced her by letting her glimpse his vulnerability.

The discovery that she was pregnant had brought his commandeering side back to the surface. But his other side had been there again in his plea to be reassured that he hadn't behaved badly.

He has good qualities, she mused. A woman

who wasn't careful could even be tricked into falling in love with him.

But I'm going to be careful, she promised herself. *Oh, yes, I am.*

CHAPTER FOUR

NEXT MORNING LEONIZIO waited for Ellie to join him at breakfast, but time passed with no sign of her. At last he knocked on her door. When this produced no response he opened it quietly and went inside.

She lay still and silent in her bed, her luscious hair spread over the pillow. Her head was turned in his direction, enabling him to see her gentle, relaxed expression. Last night she had been wretchedly agitated by whatever she had dreamed, but now peace seemed to have come over her, as though she had slipped into a kinder world.

How long would she stay in that world? And was he the demon who would destroy her peace? He was reluctant to think so.

He left the room quietly and breakfasted alone, trying to come to terms with the different signals coming from every direction.

She was a woman to confuse any man. From the first moment of knowing her he'd felt at ease with her serious mind, her businesslike efficiency, so appropriate in a lawyer.

But that had changed in a few stunning hours. Her understanding of his pain over his lost child, the sympathy he had sensed in her, these had drawn from him a reaction that had surprised even himself. He was a man who allowed few people to see inside his mind, and even fewer inside his heart. Life was safer with defences in position.

But she had seen beyond the defences, reaching out to touch him in a place where he badly needed to be touched.

The instinct to draw her closer had overcome him without warning. His arms had tightened, and their lovemaking had been just what he'd longed for.

But afterwards she'd seemed reluctant to meet his gaze, and their parting had been inevitable.

Memories of their lovemaking were still vivid. She had brought him wonderful news, but somehow she seemed to be the lawyer again. Instinctively, he had assumed that she wanted marriage, but the cool way she'd discounted it had told him much that he didn't want to know. Already she had planned the future she wanted: a life in England, her career, his place in their child's life limited to occasional visits.

As they'd dined together her manner had been pleasant but behind it he sensed her laying down the law in a way that aroused his opposition.

Years of wealth and success had accustomed him to women seeking his attention and goodwill. A woman who rejected all he had to offer despite carrying his child was a new, stunning discovery.

By the end of the evening he understood how fiercely determined she was to do things her way, and summoned in himself an equal determination not to let her get away with it.

She was right. They were combatants. He would do whatever he could to win her to his point of view, but he would always be wary of her.

But there was another surprise for him: her nightmare, the way she had clung to him, his stab of pleasure at comforting her. These had knocked him back, weakening his resolve. And the sight of her sleeping this morning had touched his heart, weakening him further.

He checked the clock. Her office would be opening about now, and it was time to get everything sorted. Ellie must marry him. On that he was determined. He picked up the phone and dialled the number of her office.

Ellie awoke to find the room already light. For a few moments she allowed herself to stretch out and relish her comfortable surroundings. At last she slipped out of bed and opened the bedroom door a crack, looking out into the corridor. On the far side was another open door, from behind which she could hear Leonizio's voice.

'I want no more delays. Get the divorce papers ready… Yes, I know it's not what I said before but I've considered the matter. Get it done, fast.'

There was the sound of a telephone being slammed down.

She closed the door and stood quietly considering what she had heard. Leonizio was intent on finalising his divorce quickly. Last night she'd told him he was close, but that wasn't enough for him. He wanted to be free to marry her and secure his child as soon as possible.

She showered, dressed and went out to meet him, expecting to find him in the grim mood suggested by his phone call. But he gave her a friendly smile.

'Did you sleep well? How do you feel this morning?'

'Fine, thank you.' She touched her stomach. 'We're both in good health.'

'Sit down while I get you some breakfast. Then we can make our plans. Today you're a tourist and I'm your guide.' He poured her coffee. 'That is, if you want to do that.'

'Oh, yes, I've always been fascinated by Rome. All that power—emperors who are famous even today. Tiberius, Caligula, Julius Caesar, Augustus, Nero, all conquering their neighbours.'

'Including your country,' Leonizio observed lightly.

'Right. You invaded Britain and ruled us for nearly four hundred years. But then we got rid of you and that was that.' She raised the coffee cup in comical salute. 'Here's to telling the Romans to push off.'

He raised his own cup. 'Here's to pushing off for a while but coming back later.'

'If we let you,' she teased.

'Yes, we'll have to see who wins that one.'

They shared a laugh and clinked cups.

'Your emperors didn't just go to war,' she mused. 'They used to murder each other. But actually—oh, thank you.'

She broke off as he set a dish before her.

'There's more right next to you,' he said. 'Yes, I think you'll enjoy the grandeur of Rome.'

She had been about to say that she was equally fascinated by another part of the city: Trastevere, the impoverished part where her grandmother had lived. But perhaps that could wait.

'Anywhere you want to start?' he asked.

'Yes, the Trevi Fountain. I've always thought it looked lovely.'

'We'll go as soon as you've finished breakfast,' Leonizio said.

When they were ready to leave, his driver was waiting. A few minutes brought them to the Trevi district, where a building almost as big as a palace rose up. In front of it was a huge pool into which water flowed, and standing just above the pool was the statue of Neptune, the Roman god of fresh water and the sea. Splendid, handsome and nearly naked, he seemed to symbolise power and authority.

Crowds had gathered around the edge of the water, including a few market stalls. One elderly woman, selling flowers, waved some of them hopefully. Leonizio purchased a small bouquet and gave it to Ellie, who received it with pleasure. It was lovely to be treated like this, even if she did know that his behaviour was calculated to win her over and gain his own way.

At the edge of the water she paused, reached into her bag for coins, and flung them into the air.

'Not like that,' Leonizio said. 'The proper way is to stand with your back to the fountain and toss the coin over your right shoulder.'

'But it might not go in properly.'

'Then you must toss another coin, to be sure. And perhaps a third.'

'Here we go.' She tossed three coins over her shoulder, but Leonizio shook his head.

'Not all together. One at a time. Do it again.'

'All right. One—two—three.'

From behind them came a cackle. Turning, Ellie saw the flower seller, convulsed with laughter.

'Never trust a man,' she said. 'He tells you to throw coins but he doesn't tell you the secret code.'

'What secret code?' Ellie asked.

'It's the legend of Trevi. One coin will bring you back to Rome. Two coins will make you fall in love with a Roman man. Three coins will make you marry him.' She cackled again. 'But perhaps you're already in love with him, and scheming to fix the wedding.'

'No such thing,' Ellie announced. 'I've never been in love in my life, and I hope I never will be. As for scheming to marry—not a chance.'

The old woman sent a crow of amusement up to the heavens.

'But he fooled you!' she cried.

A naughty imp seemed to take over Ellie's mind, making her say teasingly, 'He fools everybody. That's how he's got so many wives. They toss three coins and they all have to marry him.'

Cheers and laughter from the crowd. Leonizio regarded her wryly, partly amused, partly disconcerted at having the joke turned back on him.

'I think we should go,' he said, drawing her away.

She let him lead her to a small café in a side street.

'Very clever,' he said when they were seated. 'But did you really have to make a fool of me?'

'What about the fool you made of me? Tricking me like that.'

'Well, I've got to get you to marry me somehow, haven't I?' he said cheerfully. 'And if I have to invoke Neptune's help—that's what I'll do.'

She laughed. 'That's your code of life, isn't it? Get your own way at all costs, no matter what you have to do.'

'Are you saying your code isn't the same?'

She considered a moment before admitting, 'Exactly the same. Of course, I don't have a lot of practice—'

'You astonish me.'

'But I'm learning from you.'

'Yes, you got your revenge today, didn't you?'

'I made sure of it. Besides, where's the harm in a bit of fun?'

'No harm at all, especially if you take the other guy by surprise.'

'And it did take you by surprise, didn't it? You're not used to people fighting back.'

'I'm getting used to it with you. You obviously relished every moment.'

'I do enjoy a laugh.'

'So you think our marriage is just a joke.'

'What marriage? We're not married and who knows if we ever will be? I think it's a joke that you thought you only had to snap your fingers and I'd jump to obey. And you didn't tell me about the danger of tossing three coins.'

'Seriously, do you think I really believe that mad legend?'

'I'm not sure what I really think. This city is so different to everywhere else that I could believe impossible things. Besides which—' she regarded him ironically '—some people have a gift for making things happen. You have to be wary of them.'

'You do me an injustice. If I had anything like the power you seem to think, you would already have my ring on your finger. But I have no power at all, which is why you can keep me dancing to your tune.'

'You?' she echoed, astonished. 'You, dancing to my tune? Never.'

'I want you, Ellie, but you act like that is a crime.'

No, she thought, laying her hand gently over her stomach. *It's not me you want. If you did, everything would be different.*

'Have you really decided against me so completely?' he said. 'What have I done that offends you? Or is it that?' He indicated her stomach. 'Was that unforgivable of me?'

'Don't be melodramatic. I just haven't decided and I don't like you trying to make my decisions for me.'

'No, you like to be the one telling me what to do. Does it occur to you how alike we are? That could make a very happy marriage.'

'What, with each of us giving orders?' she demanded. 'That's not a happy marriage, it's a recipe for disaster.'

'Is that what went wrong with your parents' marriage?'

'That was a big part of it. But they didn't have the best start. They only married because they were expecting me. It wasn't what either wanted but they went ahead with it to please their parents, and were miserable together for years as a result. So, believe me, I know that isn't a good reason.'

'But wasn't there any affection between them?'

'If there was it didn't last. The air was always sharp and hostile. They made their mistakes. I'm not about to repeat them.'

Ellie stopped suddenly, her skin paling visibly as she gasped and clutched her stomach.

'What is it?' he asked urgently.

'Nothing— I just feel a bit—ooh—'

'You're nauseous, aren't you? Keep still and take deep breaths. Does it happen often?'

'Too often. I hate it. I thought pregnancy sickness only happened in the mornings.'

'It can happen any time, and it's actually something to be glad of.'

'You're kidding me.'

'No, it means that you have a lot of pregnancy hormones, and that's good news. They nourish the baby until your placenta has grown big enough to take over the job.'

She stared. 'You sound like a doctor. Have you studied medicine?'

'No, I've just trodden this path before.'

Of course he had, with his wife. Ellie could have cursed herself for her momentary forgetfulness.

'Did Harriet have a lot of sickness?' she asked.

'Plenty. She really suffered. I went to the doctor with her because I wanted to understand what she was going through, so that I could help her with the pregnancy.' He gave a wry grunt. 'There's a laugh if ever there was one.'

'It means you were a kind, considerate husband. That's not at all funny.'

'It is if I was helping her care for another man's child,' he said with a touch of wry bitterness. 'That's the biggest laugh of all time. But enough of this. You're the one who matters now.'

You mean my baby is the one that matters, she mused silently. But she suppressed the thought. Leonizio's concern was pleasant, whatever his motives.

'Let's go home,' he said. 'You need to rest.'

Taking out his cell phone, he called his driver, to summon him. A few minutes later they were on the road.

'Deep breaths,' he reminded her. 'We'll be there soon.'

In a few minutes they had reached his home. He supported her into her room, easing her down onto the bed.

'What can I get you?'

'Just a little water,' she gasped.

She drank the water he brought her, then lay down and drifted into a contented sleep. Dreams seemed to come and go. Once she had the sensation of opening her eyes to find Leonizio looking down at her anxiously. But then the mist descended again, and he vanished.

When she finally awoke the sickness had gone and she felt much better. She rose and left the room, finding him in the kitchen, cooking.

'Better?' he asked.

'Everything's fine.'

'Then you need a good meal. It'll be ready in a moment.'

She guessed this was what he had done for Harriet, caring for her when she felt poorly, feeding her to ensure she recovered properly. But he'd acted out of love for his wife, which meant Harriet had been fortunate.

How could she have betrayed a man who so loved and protected her? Ellie wondered.

But she knew the answer. It was because she hadn't returned his love.

How could she not return it? How could any woman be indifferent to such adoration?

'Are you all right?' Leonizio's voice broke into her consciousness.

'I—what did you say?'

'You had a strange look on your face—as though you were lost in a lovely dream. Or perhaps a troublesome dream.'

'A little bit of both,' she murmured.

'Care to tell me?'

'It wouldn't interest you,' she said hastily. 'You're right about supper. I'm hungry.'

She would have said anything to get him off the subject.

'Let's eat.' He led her to the table.

The light meal was delicious. As she tucked in he handed her a newspaper.

'Look at this. It lists the opera performances at the Caracalla Baths. Take your choice.'

'Lovely.'

Eagerly she scanned the paper and found one of her favourite operas being shown the following evening.

'The Barber of Seville,' she said.

'Let's hope it isn't sold out.'

He took out his mobile phone, embarked on a short conversation and gave her the thumbs-up sign.

'We're in luck,' he said. 'I think we got the last two tickets going.'

'Lovely. I'm looking forward to this.'

'There is one thing. They were very expensive seats, so you'll have to dress up to the nines. Give it everything you've got. Your most luxurious dress, your best jewellery.'

'But I haven't got anything like that with me,' she said, alarmed. 'I just came out for a quick visit with casual clothes.'

'Then we'll have to get you something suitable. There's a shop just around the corner where they sell very nice dresses. We'll go there tomorrow.'

'How much do I owe you for my ticket?'

He gave her a wry, teasing look. 'Never ask me anything like that again. It insults me, and I take terrible revenge.'

'I'll just have to risk that. You can't pay for my ticket.'

'I can if I say so. Now, be quiet, finish eating and go to bed.'

She gave a comical salute. 'Yes, sir.'

He saw her into bed, pulled the duvet up over her and kissed her cheek.

'Goodnight,' he said.

'Goodnight.'

She was glad to be alone to brood over the day's events, and the confusion they inspired in her. They had the advantage of a shared sense of humour, which enabled them to fight their battles without bitterness. Thus far, things looked hopeful, if only she could keep her feelings under control. His feelings were for the baby, not herself, and the worst thing that could happen to her would be to fall in love with him. That was something she would never allow to happen.

Finally feeling safe and content, she fell asleep.

The next morning Leonizio took her to the shop, whose window featured a dress more luxurious than she had ever dreamed of wearing. It was made of deep red satin, tight-fitting to emphasise her perfect figure. She tried it on and was left breathless with delight at the sight of herself.

'Like it?' Leonizio asked in a casual tone that suggested no real interest.

'Yes, I love it. Will it make me look suitable?'

'Hmm.' He seemed to consider the matter. 'I guess it will.'

'Then I'll— *What?*'

The exclamation of horror was torn from her as she saw the price tag.

'Oh, I've been so stupid!' she cried. 'I should

have checked that sooner. I can't afford that much.'

'You don't have to,' Leonizio said. 'I've already paid for it.'

'But—you can't have.'

Leonizio inclined his head towards a staff member standing nearby. The young woman held up her hand, revealing that it was full of notes.

'You've already paid?' Ellie said, aghast. 'But suppose I hadn't liked it?'

'Then you could have chosen something else.'

Except that he had already made his own choice, she thought. It looked like an act of generosity but actually she was being steered to do his bidding.

'Leonizio, I can't let you buy my clothes. We're not—'

'It's too soon to say what we are and what we're not. Just now you look perfect in that dress, and it's what you ought to wear.'

'Thank you,' she said in a voice that gave nothing away.

They were still playing a game, she thought. He was charming, yet she knew it was chiefly a way of overcoming her refusal.

But I can play as cunning a game as you, she thought. *Beware.*

When they returned to the apartment she donned the dress again, studying herself with satisfaction as she thought of the evening ahead. When it was time to leave, he came to find her.

'You look splendid,' he said. 'You'll do me credit.'

'And that's what matters, of course,' she said lightly.

'It matters more than you think. My business is well known in Rome, and so am I. I have a reputation to keep up.'

'And a woman who looked too ordinary would take you down a peg?'

'Exactly. I can't be seen with a lady who doesn't wear glamorous clothes and expensive jewels.'

'Then you'll have to ditch me. I have no expensive jewels.'

'Luckily, I anticipated that and took precautions.' He reached into his pocket. 'Turn around.'

She did so, and gasped as he came close behind her, raising his hands to fit a glittering diamond necklace about her neck. Ignorant as she was about jewellery, she could tell that it was worth a fortune.

'Whatever is that?' she asked breathlessly.

'My proof to the world that they needn't have doubts about me,' he said cheerfully.

She turned and saw him laughing in a way that made her heart leap.

'You're right,' she said. 'We'll flaunt it tonight and tomorrow you can take it back to the shop.'

'Hey, you're up to every trick,' he said admiringly.

'Sure I am. I could probably teach you a few.'

'Here's another one. We won't be taking this necklace back. Once I've given it you, it's yours.'

'But—'

'No buts. It's yours. My gift to you.'

'But I can't let you give me something like this.'

'Let me? Did I ask your permission?'

'You never ask my permission for any of your crazy ideas.'

'Certainly not,' he said cheerfully. 'You'd refuse, just for the pleasure of being difficult.'

'Of course. Because that's the kind of maddening woman I am.' She challenged him humorously, 'And you actually want to marry me? Are you out of your mind?'

'Probably. I've always enjoyed a challenge. And something tells me you're the biggest challenge I've ever faced. Now, stop arguing. Take the necklace and wear it for the sake of my reputation.'

She wasn't fooled. Behind his talk of reputation he'd performed a cunning manoeuvre to make her accept a luxurious gift. It was beautiful and generous. It was also a way of asserting ownership.

He stood beside her, facing the mirror.

'Will we look good together?' he asked.

Anyone would look good with such a handsome man, she thought. But she only shrugged and said lightly, 'I guess we'll pass.'

'That's all it takes. Let's go.'

CHAPTER FIVE

THE CARACALLA BATHS were unlike any other opera house in the world. The ruins of the original building provided the open-air stage, with sides marked by two vast columns. Facing it was a huge array of seats, climbing high.

'I can hardly get my head round this,' Ellie laughed as she looked around. 'Here we are to enjoy ourselves, but I looked up the Emperor Caracalla and apparently he was one of the most horrifying men who ever ruled Rome. He murdered his brother, murdered his wife and daughter, murdered anyone else who got in his way.'

'It's what emperors did two thousand years ago,' Leonizio said with a grin. 'But in the end someone murdered him.'

'Oh, that's all right then,' she chuckled. 'Fair's fair.'

She soon realised what Leonizio had meant about needing to maintain a reputation. Heads turned at the sight of him, and as he led her towards the seats nearest the stage they were greeted many times, sometimes eagerly, always respectfully. Leonizio introduced Ellie as 'a friend visiting from England'.

'Aha! Doing business in England now?' teased one man.

'But of course,' Ellie said. 'Why else would I be here?'

'It might be something to do with his weakness for a pretty face,' joked another man.

'No, no,' she assured him. 'Strictly business.'

Cheers and laughter. The murmur went around that Leonizio's latest 'friend' was shrewd and funny.

'You're a success,' Leonizio told her as he showed her to her seat. 'Strictly business, eh? Who knows?'

'Nobody. It's too soon to know.'

When everyone in the audience was settled the conductor appeared, bowed and raised his hands to conduct the overture and for the next couple of hours there was no need to talk as both Ellie and Leonizio were swept up with the drama and romance unfolding on stage—their own drama temporarily forgotten.

The performance came to a triumphant end. Smiling, the cast bowed, the audience rose and began to leave.

'Let's have a snack before we go,' he suggested.

She agreed and they headed to the theatre's bar.

'An interesting evening,' he said ironically.

'Even after watching that performance, are you still determined that you are against marriage?'

'I don't believe it's a guarantee of a happy ending.'

'True. If a couple are dazzled by unrealistic dreams they're asking for trouble. But if they're not—if their eyes are open and their thoughts realistic, they can be a success.'

'But what kind of success?'

'You said it yourself when you told my associate that we were strictly business.'

For a moment she was too taken aback to speak. Then she said, 'You think we could have a successful business relationship?'

'We each have something to offer. We arrange the terms, shake hands, and if we trust each other to keep our word it can be a successful arrangement.'

'And just what are the terms?'

'I want our child. You are carrying our baby. In return I'll provide you with a life of comfort. Whatever you want will be yours.'

'Including your fidelity?'

'If you include that in the terms.'

She considered her answer for a moment before saying casually, 'I might include a certain level of affection in the terms. But I don't think you could manage that.'

'On the contrary. My gratitude for what you have given me would ensure my warmth of feeling.'

But that's not the kind of feeling I would want, she thought. *And no life of comfort would console me for the loss.*

But there was no way she could speak such thoughts to this cool, detached man.

Assuming her most businesslike tone, she said, 'Now let me declare my terms. You can take your proper place as the child's father. Your name will be on the birth certificate, you may visit us whenever you like and establish a relationship. I promise I'll never try to shut you out, but there will be no marriage and we will not live together.'

'Meaning that we'll live in separate countries,' he declared. 'What kind of an arrangement is that?'

'The only kind I will agree to.'

He leaned back and regarded her shrewdly.

'You're a very astute businesswoman. You know you've got the power on your side and you don't concede a single point.'

'But I've conceded a lot. You'll be a real father, part of our child's life.'

'At a distance. If only you knew how much I—' He checked himself and said quickly, 'Time we were going.'

'No, finish what you were saying. If I knew how much you—?'

'It's late. You're tired. Let's go.'

She understood. He'd been on the verge of revealing the depth of his inner feelings, and he
wasn't a man who did that easily. Now he wanted
to escape her.

She was beginning to feel sleepy and it was
pleasant to let him escort her home and to her
door.

'Goodnight,' he said. 'Tomorrow we'll have
another chance to talk.'

'Yes,' she murmured. 'There's still a lot to say.
And we never know what may happen next.'

He placed his hands gently on her shoulders.
'Sleep well,' he said. 'And if you need anything,
call me.'

He backed out, closing the door firmly. He felt
a sudden need to be free of her, and the unset-
tling effect she could have on him.

There was a mysterious quality in Ellie that
tempted him to venture into dangerous territory.
He'd discovered that on the day they'd first got to
know each other, when something about her had
lured him out of his protective shell, to make love.

Since then there had been other moments when
his defensiveness had faded, alerting him to danger. Tonight he'd hovered on the brink of telling
her how much pain he suffered from the feeling
of being excluded.

It had been something he'd known all his life,

first with the family that reared him, then with the wife who had cheated on him. With the hope of a child he'd cherished a new dream: someone who belonged to him in a way that couldn't be denied. The disillusion had been an experience that made him think of hell.

He confided in nobody. That was weakness, and weakness was something he despised. But with Ellie he was tempted to yield and it alarmed him.

He stood for a while, gazing at the door that he had shut between them. Then he went back to the main room, opened the drinks cabinet and poured himself a large whisky.

He was up before her next morning, greeting her politely, making the coffee.

'You must tell me where you want to go today,' he said. 'The Colosseum, the Pantheon, more fountains?'

'It sounds wonderful. Rome is so beautiful, so grand and glorious…' Ellie paused.

'But it's not enough for you,' Leonizio ventured.

'No, if anything it's too much for me. I was hoping to see the other Rome—not the one where the emperors ruled, but where the poorer people lived.'

'Of course; you told me that your grandmother

came from Trastevere. Is that where you want to see?'

'I'd love to. But I'm not sure that you'd enjoy it.'

'You mean I'd stick out like a sore thumb?'

'No, of course not.'

He gave a wry smile. 'I think you do. When your grandmother lived in Trastevere it was a much poorer district. But now the tourists have discovered it, it's not really poor. Just lively and colourful.'

'Yes, I remember her saying that was beginning to happen.'

'Let's go to the car and we can head there first.'

'Oh, no,' she said quickly. 'I'd like to walk. We're not that far away. Trastevere is just the other side of the river, and we can get there over a footbridge.'

'The Ponte Sisto,' Leonizio murmured.

'Yes, Nonna used to say it was the loveliest way to cross the river. And the bridge isn't far from here.'

He regarded her curiously. 'You've really studied Rome, haven't you?'

'One part of it, because that's the part I've always heard about. It felt like another home, and I always promised myself I'd come here one day. I promised Nonna too, and it makes me sad that she isn't with me.'

'We'll make a good day of it,' he assured her.

'Look,' she said uneasily, 'you really don't need to come. I've studied the route. I can find my way.'

'You think you can but you'd get lost and who knows what would happen to you? The fact is you're afraid I'll spoil it, just by being there. Don't worry. I know when to back off.'

She didn't try to argue further. He was right. She was afraid that his presence would spoil everything. How could this wealthy man, so used to luxury, ever appreciate the special pleasures of Trastevere?

But she understood that he wouldn't let her out of his sight, lest some harm come to the unborn child around whom his world now revolved.

A few minutes' walk brought them to the footbridge that would take them over the Tiber River. Walking across it slowly, Ellie was able to enjoy the sight of a great hill on one side and St Peter's Basilica on the other. But at last she saw something that drove everything else out of her mind. There ahead were the tightly woven cobbled streets of Trastevere.

Soon they had left the bridge and were walking through the streets. With cobblestones underfoot and laundry hanging overhead, it was so different from the neighbourhood they had left that it might have been a new world.

Ellie walked slowly, stopping to look inside

a shop or glance upwards at the flowers that seemed to decorate every balcony. Leonizio waited for her patiently, content to let her take her pleasure in her own way. He thought wryly of other women he had entertained in Rome, flaunting the glamorous city to impress them.

But Ellie was different. He had the strange sensation that very little impressed her.

Suddenly she paused, alerted by something she had seen attached to a wall.

'What is it?' Leonizio asked.

'There—just there. The name—I can barely read it—'

He leaned close and read the name of the street.

'That's it?' she gasped. 'That's really it?'

'Yes. Does it mean something?'

'It's where Nonna used to live.'

'In one of these tiny little houses?'

'Yes. And the café must be at the end of the street. Oh, I do hope it's still there.'

'What's its name?'

'I don't know. But it was something to do with clowns.'

'Let's go.'

He took her hand and led her until they came to a place where the narrow road expanded into a square, full of shops and cafés. Although it was still before noon the place was full of life. The shops were open, the cafés had tables out on the pavements. Music and laughter floated through the air.

'Oh, it's lovely,' Ellie breathed. 'But can you see any clowns?'

'I think so,' Leonizio said. 'Over there.' He pointed to a café on the corner with a notice that read, 'Casa dei Pagliacci'.

'Is your Italian good enough for that?'

'Oh, yes!' she cried in delight. 'It means Home of the Clowns.'

He took her hand. 'Let's go.'

As soon as they entered she knew she was going to love this place. Clowns were everywhere. Pictures of them covered the walls, and the waiters were all colourfully dressed as clowns.

The place was crowded, with just one unoccupied table, which they approached quickly. A waiter danced up to them, showed them a menu and bounced away.

'It's like nowhere I've ever been before,' she breathed.

They were just enjoying a light lunch when suddenly there was the sound of cheering. A musician dressed as a clown appeared, bearing a guitar, and began to play. He was joined by another clown, who did a little dance and sang a cheeky ballad. The crowd applauded and he bowed theatrically, travelling around the tables, gesturing to everyone and accepting their gifts.

The first clown went on singing, bowing elaborately when the crowd applauded. Ellie clapped excitedly and the clown approached her, performing theatrically, evidently enjoying her contribution. When they had finished everyone applauded and the clown gazed at her.

'Do you know this song?' he asked.

'My grandmother used to sing it,' Ellie said. 'She came from here.'

'From here? From Trastevere?'

'She lived nearby and she knew this very café. She had friends here.'

'What was her name?'

'Lelia Basini.'

The clown stared in amazement. 'Lelia? You are Lelia's granddaughter? Oh, yes, you must be. Your face is so like hers.'

Now she could see him more closely, and realised that beneath the clown's make-up he was an old man.

'Sit down and talk to us,' Leonizio invited. 'What is your name?'

'I am called Marco. And it is a pleasure to meet Lelia's granddaughter. Is Lelia still alive?'

'Sadly no. It's a long time since she was here,' Ellie said. 'Did you really know her?'

'Oh, yes. I was a waiter here in those days. There were many young men who courted her, and she flirted with us all, but not seriously. She fell in love with another man and went to England. We had only the pictures she left us as memories.'

'Pictures?'

'We all had our photographs taken with her, so that we could keep and treasure them.'

'You have photographs of her?' Ellie breathed. 'Are any of them here? Can I see them?'

'I'll go and find out.'

He returned a few minutes later with a large folder that he laid on the table before Ellie.

'These pictures belong to my great friend, Paolo. He also knew your grandmother well,' he said. 'He doesn't keep them at home in case his wife finds them.'

'After so many years?' Leonizio queried.

'Yes, indeed,' Marco agreed. 'He was very much under Lelia's spell.'

'I can see why,' Leonizio observed.

The girl in the pictures was no beauty but she had a charm and personality that glowed even through the old black-and-white photographs. She laughed, she met the eyes of the men she was with. She was an enchantress.

'Do you recognise her?' Leonizio asked.

'I remember her as a lot older, but yes, it's the same face. And something about her smile never changed over the years.'

'And you are very like her,' Marco said. He addressed Leonizio. '*Signore*, you are a lucky man.'

'Believe me, I know it.'

'Was she happy in England?' Marco asked.

'Oh, yes, my grandparents were happily married.'

'I'm glad she was happy,' Marco said, adding theatrically, 'No man here was happy without her. Ah, but I must leave you.'

He made as if to gather up the pictures, but Ellie fended him off.

'Let me look at them a little longer,' she begged.

When he'd gone she went through the pictures again, entranced by this new view of Lelia.

'I don't believe this is happening,' she said in a daze.

'We were right to come here,' Leonizio said. 'You're a different person in these surroundings.'

'Different? How?'

'You're more relaxed, as though you felt at home here in a way you haven't before.'

'I hoped it would be a nice day,' she said happily, 'but I couldn't have hoped for anything like this. I have the strangest feeling that Nonna is here somewhere; like a ghost haunting me.'

'Not a ghost,' Leonizio said gently. 'She really is with you, here—' he touched her forehead '—and here.' He laid his hand over her breast.

'She's still in your mind and your heart, and I think she always will be.'

It was true, she realised. But what surprised her most was that Leonizio had been able to see it.

She realised that her knowledge of him was limited. His mind and his feelings went deeper than she had understood.

'Just a moment,' he said. 'I've thought of something.'

He rose and left her, heading for the door through which Marco had disappeared. Ellie barely noticed him go. She had found one picture that seemed to speak to her more than any other.

In it Lelia sat alone, smiling at the camera, her gaze full of a kind of cheeky charm that Ellie remembered well from her childhood.

'Oh, how I miss you,' she murmured. 'We understood each other. If only—'

She stopped as she saw Leonizio approaching her with Marco.

'He says you can have any of the pictures you like,' Leonizio said. 'Just take your pick.'

'You mean—?'

'Whatever you want,' Marco said.

Her heart leapt with happiness. 'Can I take this one?' she said, holding up the picture that had entranced her.

Marco nodded. 'You are welcome to keep it,' he said.

He backed away, but not before Ellie had noticed him reaching out to take something from Leonizio's hand. She couldn't see exactly what passed between them, but she reckoned she knew. Astonished, she looked up at Leonizio as Marco left them.

'Did you pay him?' she gasped.

'Just a little. I could see what those pictures meant to you. I thought you should have at least one.' He added wryly, 'Of course I did it without consulting you, which doubtless condemns me as a bully. You might want to take some revenge.'

'And how would I do that?' she said, smiling.

'It's up to you. I suppose you could thump me.'

'Mmm. I'm sure I could think of something more interesting. In the meantime, I'll just say thank you. It's a lovely thing to have.'

She gazed at the photograph, eyes shining with pleasure. Leonizio regarded her, fascinated. He thought of something else he'd given her, the luxurious diamond necklace. He'd offered costly gifts to women before and they had seized on them as the natural spoils from a rich man. But this woman cared nothing for expensive jewels. She had even tried to reject the diamonds. It was a memento of her grandmother that made her happy.

This was his chance to get closer to her, Leonizio realised. Ellie had let her guard down around him for the first time since arriving in Italy. When they got home they could talk more freely than before, and everything would be different. By the end of the day she might even have agreed to marry him.

'Perhaps we should go home now,' he said. 'You're looking tired.'

'Yes, let's go.'

'And this time we're taking a taxi. No arguments.'

'All right. Whatever you say.'

He grinned. 'Now you've got me really worried. When you speak in that submissive way I wonder what you're planning. I guess I'll have to wait and see.'

She chuckled but made no reply in words. He paid the bill, adding a substantial tip to reflect his pleasure in the way the lunch had turned out, and led her out.

In the taxi she leaned back, sighing with pleasure. 'That was lovely,' she said.

'Yes, wasn't it? But the day doesn't have to end now. We could go somewhere else this evening.'

'Actually, Leonizio, I'm rather worn out. If you don't mind, I would like to rest up this afternoon and evening. And I should really check in with the office. I'm sure that my work is really piling up back in London. But thank you for taking me there.'

Back at his apartment, she touched his arm gently and went into her room, leaving him standing there, reflecting on how wrong he'd been to think they could have an affectionate talk.

It was true, he thought wryly, that the day had aroused her warmer feelings.

But not for him.

CHAPTER SIX

THE NEXT MORNING Leonizio was already up, making the coffee. He greeted Ellie with a smile when she wandered into the kitchen.

'Did you have a good night?'

'A lovely night. I felt Nonna and I were back together, talking as we used to.'

'Did she say anything interesting?'

'Oh, yes. She's so wise. She helps me see everything differently. I want to remember seeing her street, the house she once lived in and going to that café. It was such a happy day. Did it seem that way to you? Or isn't Trastevere your kind of place?'

'What makes you think that? Why shouldn't it be?'

'Well, since you made your fortune don't you live a more high society life?'

'You think I'm too lofty? You couldn't be more wrong. Trastevere is very much my kind of place, and I know it well. My uncle owned a little shop there, and he made such a success of it that he managed to buy another shop. I used to earn pocket money being his messenger boy.'

He grinned. 'And not just him. A lot of the other shops used me to run errands—for a price. Those were good times. I had a lot of friends there.

'In fact I still have friends who live there. Taking you there yesterday made me realise how long it's been since I've seen some of them. In fact I quite fancy looking up some of my old friends.' A thought seemed to strike him. 'Do you fancy coming with me?'

'Oh, yes, I'd love to.'

'We'll go tonight then. Do you want to do some more exploring this afternoon?'

'I'd like to see the Pantheon.'

'That's where we'll go.'

After the Pantheon they took a stroll through the streets. Ellie found Rome so beautiful that just wandering about was a pleasure. Escorting her, Leonizio was alert for anything that might interest her.

'Over there you'll see— Ellie? Ellie—where are you?'

Looking around, he saw that he had completely lost her attention. She had moved away and was gazing ecstatically into a shop window at a collection of shoes.

'I've heard that Italian shoes are lovely,' she said. 'And these really are. Especially those.' She indicated a pair in the centre of the display. 'I'm going in to try them on. Hey, let me go.'

Leonizio had put his arm about her waist, holding her back.

'Don't move,' he said, smiling. 'You're not going in there.'

'Why? Is something wrong with those shoes?'

'No, the pair you're looking at are Fellani shoes.'

'Fellani? Yours? Really?'

'From our latest range. Come to the factory and see.'

She agreed, eager to see the factory, which she felt would tell her so much about him.

In half an hour they had reached a large building near the edge of the city. Looking at the windows, Ellie saw faces which lit up at the sight of him.

Inside, there were machines everywhere, making buzzing noises. A young man came to meet them.

'My assistant, Francesco,' Leonizio said.

He introduced them, explaining that Ellie was a lawyer, and a friend. On his instructions, Francesco fetched a collection of shoes, which Leonizio proceeded to fit on her feet. The ones she liked best were the ones she had seen in the shop, but they were too small.

'I'm afraid we don't have a larger size here at the moment,' Francesco said.

'Then we'll make a pair specially,' Leonizio said.

They proceeded to examine Ellie's feet.

'I hadn't expected this,' she said when Francesco had left them. 'How much do I owe you?'

'Owe me? You surely don't think I'm going to charge you? You're a special guest.'

'But the shoes look expensive and I sort of forced this on you,' she said, embarrassed.

'Do you really think you could force anything on me against my will?'

'Well, if you put it that way—I guess I couldn't. But I'm honoured. A pair made especially for me. Wow!'

'You're not just an ordinary customer.'

His voice was warm and she wondered if she'd only imagined that his glance fell on her stomach.

But of course, she thought. It was her pregnancy that made her special. He had never pretended otherwise. But still his care of her was heart-warming.

When it was settled that the shoes would be delivered next day they left to finish the journey to Trastevere.

As they went through the streets Ellie recognised some of the places they had passed the day before. Leonizio stopped outside a little shop.

'This was the first one my uncle owned,' he said. 'He made a success out of it but it took all his energy.'

The shop was tiny and narrow, selling everything at low prices.

'Did you ever work for him in here?' she asked.

'Yes, for hours. And I promised myself I'd escape and make a different life.'

'You certainly did that,' she laughed. 'Is there anyone who hasn't heard of the powerful Leonizio Fellani?'

He grinned. 'I hope not. Of course, some of them disapprove of me.'

'Naturally. If you've got the better of them they'll curse you, but that just means you're a success.'

'Ellie, you have the soul of a true businesswoman.'

'So I should hope,' she said cheerfully. 'Life's more fun that way.'

'Hey, Leonizio!'

The cry made Ellie look round at the man waving and making his way towards them.

'Ottimo per vedere di nuovo.'

Ellie just recognised the words as 'Great to see you again.' Leonizio greeted him, introduced her and said, 'Speak English for my friend. Ellie, this is Nico.'

'It is a pleasure to meet you,' Nico said, taking her hand. 'In fact it's always a pleasure to meet one of Leonizio's lovely ladies.'

'Be careful,' Leonizio warned.

'Don't worry,' Ellie said. 'I doubt he could tell

me anything I haven't already worked out. And I am only your lawyer.' She faced him, smiling. 'Aren't I?'

Leonizio's face betrayed his confusion. 'Whatever you say.'

'Ah, then all is well!' Nico exclaimed in relief. 'Now let me take you for a coffee.'

'I don't think—' Leonizio began.

'That's a lovely idea,' Ellie said. 'I could just do with a coffee.'

As they left the shop Leonizio whispered in her ear, 'You're enjoying this, aren't you?'

'More than you'll ever imagine,' she agreed.

There was a small café next door. When they were settled, Nico ordered for them before saying, 'Hey, look who's over there!'

Another man was waving to them from the far side of the room. He too seemed familiar with Leonizio, signalling him to come over.

'Go and say hello,' Nico said. 'After all, you owe them.'

Leonizio glowered at him but went across to the couple, both of whom embraced him heartily.

'He owes them?' Ellie queried.

'Yes, but not money,' Nico chuckled. 'A favour. Something to do with a young lady. It was several years ago. In those days Leonizio was a *libertino*, a rather wild young man.'

'You mean wild where women are concerned?' Ellie queried. 'Libertine is an English word too.'

'Ah, yes. He often created trouble for himself, and they gave him an alibi for—well, I don't know the details. It was before he got married and became middle-aged.'

'Middle-aged? He's only thirty-four.'

'On the outside. Inside, he's grim and ferocious and years older than he actually is.'

'I see what you mean. So he has quite a history?'

'They say he had his pick of all the girls in Rome, and sometimes he seemed to pick them all. And they picked him. But then he fell in love with this English lady and became a different man—at least for a while. I heard a rumour that he was divorcing her for infidelity.'

'That's true.'

'Then he must have turned into a different man again. Who can say who he is now?'

She nodded, but did not reply. Nico had struck a nerve. Who could say who Leonizio was now? Perhaps he didn't even know himself.

'Have you known him long?' she asked.

'I used to work in the shop when his uncle owned it. I hated that man. So did most people. Cold, hard, indifferent to everyone but himself. When Leonizio inherited it I worked for him, which was much more pleasant. He's a hard man but a generous employer. Then I managed to raise the money to buy it. Ah, here he is.'

Leonizio returned and now they were able to settle down together for the evening. Ellie was fascinated. She was seeing new sides to Leonizio and he intrigued her more every moment.

As they left the building he said in a cheerful voice, 'I guess I don't have any reputation left.'

'Why should you think that?'

'I overheard some of what Nico said, especially *libertino*.'

She laughed. 'Well, you never pretended to be a man of strict virtue. Actually, Nico said some very nice things about you. According to him, you're better than your uncle, who was cold, hard, indifferent to everyone but himself.'

'True enough. Growing up with him and my aunt was like growing up without any family. I used to envy the other kids who had parents who visited their school, got involved, came to see them in the school play.'

'They didn't come to see you in the—?'

'Why should they bother? They cared nothing for me.'

'But if you were your uncle's heir, mustn't he have had some feelings for you to make such a will?'

'He didn't make a will. My aunt died before him and his possessions came to me as his closest living relative. I was grateful for the lucky stroke of fate, but—well—' He shrugged.

But there had been no emotional comfort in his inheritance, she realised.

'Never mind.' He put his arm around her. 'I have a family now.'

'Yes,' she said. 'Yes, you do.'

'And it means more than money ever could.'

'As long as it makes you happy.'

'Happy? There are no words for how happy I am. I didn't believe it was possible.'

She looked down at her still flat stomach, caressing it gently.

'Do you hear that?' she asked their unseen companion. 'Your daddy is already crazy about you. Aren't you lucky?'

'I'm the one who's lucky,' Leonizio said. He addressed her belly. 'Are you listening? I'll always come to your school play. That's a promise.'

Ellie laughed and hugged him. In the taxi on the way home she leaned her head on his shoulder, wondering when she had ever felt such a sense of peaceful contentment.

Several pairs of shoes were delivered next morning. She tried them all on, enchanted by their beauty and comfort.

'They're lovely,' she said.

'Glad you like them.' Leonizio grinned. 'Now I know that our customers will like them.'

'Oh, I see. I'm a marketing experiment.'

'You don't mind, do you?'

'Not at all. I hope I'm a success.'

They both laughed, and he said, 'We'll drop by the factory and let them see you wearing them. They'll love it.'

He was right. The workers cheered when she arrived. Francesco took a load of photographs of her feet.

'They'll make great advertisements,' he said.

'You might end up with a modelling fee,' Leonizio teased her.

She stayed at the factory the rest of the morning and had lunch with him in the works canteen.

'Oh, I'm loving this,' she sighed. 'I don't know when I've enjoyed a holiday so much.'

'Is that what I am to you?' he asked ironically. 'A holiday?'

'No, I didn't mean— It was just—'

Words failed her. There was no way to express what they both knew, that they were getting to know each other to see how the future would work out. The more she enjoyed Rome, the more confused she became. Her life was settled, and how much Leonizio would be a part of it was something she still couldn't decide.

But she'd be wise to remember one thing. Leonizio was taking wonderful care of her, but chiefly because he wanted something. And she was hovering dangerously on the edge of being fooled.

It was time to escape.

'I really must leave Rome and get back to work,' she said uneasily.

'So soon? Can't you stay a little longer?'

'No, there are things I have to do—I can't just neglect my job. This has been lovely but—'

He shrugged. 'All right, let it go. I know what you're really telling me. We'll both go to England. I want to be there to see my divorce become final as soon as possible, and sign anything I need to sign.'

'Yes, it will all be simpler if you're there.'

'I must stay here for a few hours now and fix things so that they can manage without me while I'm away.'

'I'll get out of your way. I can go home and watch the news on television, and see if my Italian is good enough to follow it.'

'Fine. I'll see you this evening. I'll send for the car.'

'No need. I can walk back. It's not far, and I like to explore.'

She enjoyed the stroll through the streets. At home she put her feet up and watched the television, then took up a newspaper that had been delivered and began to read it. She found that she understood more than she had expected.

Perhaps I should try reading a book, she thought. *Let's see.*

She began to browse, remembering seeing Leonizio glancing through a large volume about Rome, which he had finally put away on a tall shelf. Searching, she found it easily and reached up to take it down. But her movements dislodged other books on either side. She grabbed them quickly, but one fell to the floor. She dropped down beside it, suddenly tense at what she could see. The book had fallen open at a page that contained a photograph of a man and a woman, dressed for a wedding.

Only half believing what her eyes told her, Ellie studied the man's face and realised that it was Leonizio. He was looking at his bride—this must be Harriet—with an expression of love. She looked up at him, not with love but with a teasing expression.

Had there really been so much difference between them? Ellie wondered. She could easily believe it. The story of their marriage and Harriet's deception suggested that she had seen him as a man she could use.

There were more pictures in the album. Absorbed, Ellie went through it, watching the couple enjoying each other's company in many different ways. One picture of them relaxing on a beach showed Leonizio in a pair of swim shorts that showed off his shape: slim but muscular, perfectly proportioned.

Could any woman look at that body without wanting to take it to bed? Ellie wondered. The memories it revived in her were achingly beautiful.

There was a brief letter enclosed, from the friend who had taken the pictures.

Thought you'd like to see how they came out. Nice to see you and Harriet so happy. Here's to your future.

Browsing through the rest of the album, Ellie grew very still when she came to another picture. The couple were sitting together with his hand on her stomach. Again he wore a look of adoration, but this time it was clearly for the baby, and the happiness he was sure would soon be his.

The sight of his face hurt her. It was so vulnerable in his belief that his dreams had come true. Ellie had always known that the truth had hurt him, but now she could sense how brutally his heart had been broken.

And so he now clung to her, she mused. Because in her he sensed a chance to revive his hopes. She couldn't blame him, despite the ache of regret that this was the only reason he valued her.

At last something in the silence made her look up to find Leonizio standing there, his eyes fixed on her.

'I'm sorry,' she said hastily. 'I didn't mean to pry. I just came across this accidentally.'

'Don't worry,' he said. 'I guess you know about that part of my life.'

'Yes, and I'm glad to understand you a little better.'

'How do you mean?'

'I've heard you talk about Harriet with something like hate in your voice. I hadn't realised how deeply you once felt about her.'

'You don't think love can turn into hate? On the contrary. The deeper the love, the deeper the hate.'

He spoke quietly but there was a violence of feeling in his eyes. This was a man who had not merely felt a mild affection. He had loved with an intensity that had put his life on the line.

She wondered how it would feel to inspire such feelings.

'What about you?' he asked. 'Don't you know how it feels to hate?'

'No. Nobody has ever mattered that much.'

'What about the guy you told me about, who left you for another woman?'

'I put him behind me. When I decided that he no longer existed—that's when he ceased to exist.'

'You make it sound so easy.'

'It can be, if you really want it to be.'

As she watched, the intensity vanished from his face, leaving it blank.

'It will happen to you one day,' he said quietly. 'Someone will become your life to such an extent that when they betray you there's nothing left.'

She shivered. He had driven all feeling out, leaving only emptiness inside himself, and somehow he troubled her more this way.

'Nothing?' she asked.

'Nothing.'

Suddenly she heard her cell phone ringing from another room. She headed out but turned in the doorway, meaning to speak to him. But what she saw held her silent.

Leonizio was looking at a picture of Harriet, and Ellie thought she had never seen so much sadness in anyone's face. He didn't move, but sat with his eyes fixed on the woman who had illuminated his life, then destroyed it. Only a moment ago his face had been blank and empty. Now it was haunted by despair.

She hesitated, longing to speak to him but fearful lest any word from her would be ill-chosen. While she tried to decide, the telephone shrilled again and she hurried away to her room.

It was her boss on the phone.

'OK,' he said. 'We've got the final papers.'

She drew a sharp breath. 'Everything?'

'Everything. Best get back here fast, both of you.'

'Yes. I'll call you back when I've spoken to him.' She hung up.

Leonizio appeared in the doorway.

'Has something happened?' he asked tensely.

'That was Alex. You were right about coming to England. We're in the final stage.'

'Great. Let's be on our way.'

'I'll check some good London hotels, although I'm sure you already know the best.'

'Hotels?' he said. 'That's a very unkind suggestion. I'd hoped you were going to invite me to stay with you.' He gave a brief laugh. 'If you could see your face! I guess I know what you think of that suggestion.'

'It's only that my place is small. I don't have another bed.'

'Do you have a sofa?'

'Well, yes, but—'

'Then I'll sleep on the sofa. And I'll do my share of tidying up. Don't argue. It's settled.'

A combination of exasperation and amusement made her say, 'There's really no getting rid of you, is there?'

'That depends how much you want to get rid of me.'

She gave him a teasing look. 'Perhaps I haven't quite made up my mind.'

'Let me help you.'

Dropping his hands on her shoulders, he drew her close enough to lay his mouth against hers. It wasn't a passionate kiss, but a gentle assertion of possession, lasting just long enough to make his point.

'Does that make it any easier?' he asked.

She considered. 'Not really. Some things are hard to decide.'

'I could try again—with your permission, of course.'

Oh, he was a cunning so-and-so, she reckoned: putting the decision on her.

'All right,' she said, 'but try to do better this time.'

That would provoke him, she thought. His next kiss would be fiercer, more determined.

But his lips only brushed her mouth even more softly than before.

'Get rid of me later,' he murmured. 'For the moment I'm coming with you to England.'

Without waiting for her reply, he turned away to the telephone and called the airport.

Ellie clenched her fists, alarmed at her own reaction. She'd been ready for the second kiss to be passionate, and its restraint had left her heart beating fiercely with disappointment.

She stepped back, annoyed with him for disappointing her, but even more annoyed with herself for caring.

'The plane leaves this afternoon at four o'clock,' Leonizio said, hanging up. 'I've bought us tickets.'

'How much do I owe you?'

'Nothing. I'll pay for your ticket.'

'Thank you, but no. I pay for my own ticket. I don't ask you to support me.'

He seemed about to argue, but changed his mind, muttering, 'I'll go and pack.'

'Me too.'

She left him quickly, lest he see how disturbed she was. The touch of his lips had aroused an eagerness for another, deeper kiss. She had resisted it, but was dismayed at herself for feeling it at all.

And why had he picked that particular moment to kiss her? Just a few minutes ago Harriet had intruded on his consciousness, reviving thoughts and feelings that disturbed him. Had he turned to her in genuine desire? Or was it an act of defiance against the past, against Harriet?

Whatever the answer, she must struggle harder to be in control of the situation. She had promised herself that control. But it wasn't working as she'd planned.

Was there any way of coping with this infuriating man?

There was no chance to brood further. Now the time was taken up with practical matters: packing, getting to the airport, boarding the plane.

'The flight will be two and a half hours,' he said, 'and it will be late by the time we reach your place. So let's eat plenty on the plane.'

He was right. By the time they landed and left the airport the light was fading. It took another hour for the taxi to reach London and start the journey to her home. At first they travelled through the expensive part of town, but gradually the streets grew shabbier.

At last they pulled up near a five-storey block of flats. Leonizio looked up high.

'You live there?'

'Yes, I'm in one of the top apartments.'

Inside, they headed for the elevator, but got no further. A notice announced that it was out of order.

'Oh, no!' Ellie groaned. 'It was supposed to be mended by now. Oh, well, up we go.'

She headed for the stairs, followed by Leonizio, who took her suitcase as well as his own.

'You can't carry them both,' she protested. 'They'll be much too heavy.'

He grinned. 'Nonsense. Superman can carry any weight. Lead on.'

She began to climb the stairs, going slowly. About half way up she paused, taking deep breaths.

'You shouldn't be doing a climb like this,' he said. 'It's taking too much out of you.'

'Nonsense, I'm Superwoman.'

'But Superwoman needs Superman.'

They had reached a corner where the stairs flattened out into a wide ledge. Leonizio dumped the suitcases and reached out to her.

'Come here,' he said. And the next moment she was lifted high in his arms.

'Direct me,' he demanded.

'Two more flights and then we're at my front door.'

He mastered the two flights quickly, setting her down by the door while he went back for the cases. She hurried inside, wondering what would happen now.

The way he'd lifted her without checking her feelings left her in two minds.

Chivalrous? she mused. Or controlling? Or perhaps they were two halves of the same.

But she had to admit she didn't mind being saved the effort of climbing the last stairs.

He appeared with the cases and looked around.

She wondered how he would regard her plain little apartment after the glamorous luxury of his own home. He'd chosen to sleep on the sofa, but that was before he'd seen how narrow and hard it was.

'You'd really better go to a hotel,' she said. 'You can't sleep on that sofa.'

'I'll be fine. I'm staying here. No arguments. My mind is made up.'

'All right, I'll get you some blankets.'

She did her best to make him comfortable, fetching some blankets and a pillow, then arranging them on the sofa.

'Can I have that?' he asked, pointing to a small table. 'And a lamp? I like to read at night.'

She put the table where he indicated, near his head, and set a small metal lamp on it.

'So what's the next step?' he asked. 'When do I sign the papers?'

'I'll call my boss. Luckily, I've got his home number.'

Alex Dallon answered the phone at once.

'We're here,' she said.

'You don't mean you actually managed to make Fellani see sense? Well done, Ellie. You've got a great career in front of you.'

Leonizio glanced up and she realised with dismay that Dallon's voice was loud and sharp enough to carry beyond the phone.

'Shut up!' she said desperately.

'Get him in here tomorrow,' Dallon continued. 'Drag him if you have to.'

'Goodnight,' she said desperately and hung up before he could say more.

To her relief, Leonizio was grinning.

'You won't have to drag me,' he assured her.

'I'm sorry. He had no right to speak of you like that.'

'Especially when I'm near enough to overhear him. Don't worry, it's not your fault. And in a way he was right. You have helped me to see sense about some things.' His tone became ironic. 'You might say there are things I'm trying to get you to see sense about. Except that so far I'm not doing well.'

'I'll ignore that remark,' she said lightly.

'Very wise. We both have to sort out our brains before anything more happens. The problem is that we don't agree what "seeing sense" means.'

'We'll have to wait and discover how things turn out. We don't know each other very well yet.'

'Don't we? Wasn't there one moment when we knew each other very well indeed?'

'No,' she said softly. 'We thought we did, but— well—it was…'

'An illusion,' he sighed.

'I think so.'

'The trouble is, there are some illusions you want to cling to.'

'But it isn't always a good idea,' she said.

'True. Or it can be a wonderful idea.'

'But if it's only an illusion—'

'Then we could work to make it reality. What is an illusion, what is reality? Is there really a difference?'

It could be so tempting to follow him along this path, she thought. But it was a temptation she must resist, and it would be better to escape him now.

'Can I get you anything before you settle for the night?' she asked politely.

'No, thank you. Just don't vanish without warning.'

'Promise.'

She left him and hurried to her own room. It felt like taking refuge, so troublesome did she find him these days. There she could enjoy the sensation of relaxing, free from the world. Poor and shabby her apartment might be, but to her it was home in a way that nowhere else ever had been. She had found it when she went to work for Alex Dallon, knowing that she had defeated four other applicants for the job. It was her independence, her success, her right to be herself, think her own thoughts, travel her own path.

She knew Leonizio had seen only its disadvantages. He would never understand her thoughts or dreams, and perhaps for that reason they would never be truly close.

CHAPTER SEVEN

ELLIE SETTLED CONTENTEDLY in bed and managed to get to sleep quickly, but awoke after a while with the night only partly over.

She wondered how Leonizio was managing next door. She could hear some faint creaking which went on for several minutes, suggesting that he was tossing and turning restlessly. She understood that very well. What was happening to them now was disturbing.

Suddenly there came a loud clatter and the sound of crashing. Hurriedly, she jumped up and dashed into the other room.

Leonizio was lying on the floor, looking stunned. Beside him lay the metal lamp.

'I fell off,' he growled. 'And I knocked your lamp down. Sorry.'

For a moment she couldn't respond. He had removed all clothes but for a pair of boxers. The sight of him almost naked made her draw a sharp breath.

He tried to hoist himself back onto the sofa, but gave up.

'My arm,' he growled. 'I landed on it. Ouch!'

'Let me help you,' she said. 'Put your other arm around me.'

He did so. She wrapped her arms about him and together they managed to lift him the few inches onto the sofa.

'Thanks,' he growled, dropping his head and beginning to rub it.

'Is your head injured?' she asked anxiously.

'No, just a little bump. I'll be all right in a moment.'

'Can I get you something?'

'No, I'll just go back to sleep.'

'Not here. This sofa is too small for you. You must sleep in my bed.'

'You mean—?'

'I'll sleep on the sofa. I'm small enough to fit on there. Come along. Don't argue.'

'Yes, ma'am.'

Leaning on her, he rose to his feet and let her support him into the bedroom and onto the bed, where he stretched out with a sigh of relief.

'I'm supposed to be here looking after you,' he sighed. 'You could say I'm making a mess of it.'

'No, you couldn't. Stop making a drama out of a little accident.'

He regarded her wryly. 'Well, you did warn me the sofa was too small. I should have listened.'

'You? Listen to advice? Don't make me laugh.'

'All right, all right. I give in.'

'That's what I like to hear.' She pulled the covers up over him. 'Now, go to sleep.'

He snuggled down and closed his eyes. After a moment she retreated into the other room. There she lay down on the sofa and tried to go back to sleep.

But sleep eluded her. Her mind was filled with visions she didn't want to see, and thoughts she didn't want to indulge.

She had made love with this man, but until tonight she hadn't seen him nearly naked. His smooth, muscular torso, narrow hips and long elegant legs had come as a shock. Even more stunning had been the sudden urgent desire to wrap her arms about his naked flesh, holding it against her, enjoying the sensation.

But it was a losing battle. The feel of his body had been so thrilling that it haunted her still, inflaming her anger and defiance.

She had vowed to fend off his attempts to take control of her, and she could manage that where it concerned him giving her orders. But there was no protection against the surges of temptation that he could inspire against her will. She could only determine not to let him suspect.

She was up early the next morning, preparing breakfast, wondering how Leonizio would cope with everything that was to happen that day.

When he appeared she was shocked at the bruise on his forehead.

'I hit the lamp a bit harder than I thought,' he said, reading her expression. 'But it's all right. Your colleagues will think you've started beating me up already.'

She didn't query 'already', guessing that it was a hint about the marriage he was still trying to talk her into.

'I'll pick my own moment for that,' she said lightly. 'Eat up, then we'll get going.'

When they reached her office Alex Dallon was engaged with another client. While they waited for him, Leonizio stood by the window, gazing out at a row of shops over the road.

'That department store over the street stocks Fellani shoes.'

Ellie looked up at him and smiled. 'Your shoes are very desirable to the UK market.'

He nodded. 'Some of my best sales are in England. It's worth thinking about.'

'Sorry to keep you waiting,' came a voice from behind them.

They turned to see Alex, holding a sheaf of papers.

'I expect Ellie's told you how close we are to the finish,' he said. 'Your wife applied to the court for what's known as a 'quickie divorce' and a few brief formalities will tie up all the loose ends.'

He handed Leonizio the papers, which he sat down to read. Ellie went to sit beside him.

'You'd better go through them for me,' Leonizio said. 'I'm not sure my English is up to it.'

She did her duty, explaining as she went, making sure he knew how completely final this was. Remembering how the picture of Harriet had affected him, Ellie wondered how this would make him feel, but he listened with a blank, unresponsive face.

'And when I sign these papers, that's it?' he said.

'There will be no barriers to divorce,' Alex said. 'And it will be granted in a few days. You'll be completely free.'

'Thank you,' Leonizio said in a toneless voice. 'Now I must go. Send me your bill and I'll pay it at once.'

He headed for the door. Alex indicated for her to follow him and she did so, gladly. Something told her that Leonizio shouldn't be alone just now.

They found a restaurant with tables in a small garden. Leonizio ordered coffee for her and whisky for himself.

'I need a drink,' he said. 'So that's tied up all the ends. Now Harriet has her divorce it leaves her free to marry her lover before they have their child.'

'Don't,' Ellie pleaded. 'I know it's hard for you,

but let her go. Let the baby go. Don't grieve for the rest of your life.'

'But what am I supposed to do? Forget grief because it's inconvenient?'

'No, I suppose not,' she sighed.

It hurt her to see his air of defeat. It was as though all life and hope had ended for him.

'That's it,' he said. 'All done. All over.'

'Not over,' she said. 'You haven't lost everything.' She took his hand and laid it on her stomach. 'You still have this.'

'Do I?'

'Yes. This baby is yours and nothing will ever change that.'

'Does that mean you'll marry me now that I'm a free man?'

'It means it doesn't matter whether we marry or not. You'll have a relationship with your child whatever happens. Marriage isn't everything. I can give you a great deal without that.'

He made a wry face and took a sip of whisky.

'I'll be going now,' he said. 'I mustn't keep you from your work. I'll see you at home tonight.'

'You'd better have your key,' she said, reaching into her purse. 'I got you a spare before we left this morning, so you can come and go without me.'

'Thanks. And thank you for—for everything.'

He departed so quickly that she sensed he desperately needed to get away.

For the rest of the day she tried to concentrate on work, but it was hard when she couldn't help thinking of Leonizio, wandering alone, brooding bitterly on the feeling that his life was over.

Unless I agree to marry him, she thought. *It would be so easy to say yes, but I just can't. He has no feelings for me. Only for our baby and his other life. Could I bear to live with that?*

No. She couldn't face it. It would be easy to develop feelings for Leonizio, and that was a reason for not marrying him. It would mean a life of misery and jealousy.

At last the day was over and she could return home.

'I'm here,' she called as she entered.

Silence.

'Hello, Leonizio. I'm home.'

But there was no reply. She wandered through the rooms, seeking him, finding only emptiness, while her heart sank.

Where was he? What was he doing that had taken him so long? Now she recalled that when he had left her in the café he'd had an air of purpose.

But what could his purpose be?

Was it possible that he had gone to seek Harriet, determined to have one more meeting with her?

Was his love for her really as dead as he thought? Had he discovered renewed feelings that made it vital for him to see her again? He had spoken of the link between love and hate. Had his hate taken a new direction?

No, she told herself. That was absurd fantasy. He would return soon.

But an hour passed without any sign of Leonizio. Glancing out of the window, she saw an empty street.

Now she knew she had no choice but to accept the truth. She could only go to bed, not on the sofa, as she had previously decided, but in her own bedroom, since he would not be coming back. There she lay in silent desperation until at last she fell asleep.

She awoke in the early hours to find the apartment still silent. She knew at once that he had not returned. He was out there, making the plans that suited him, ignoring her wishes, thinking only of his own.

And what are his wishes? she wondered. *If I give in and do whatever he wants, what happens then? He doesn't care for me. I'm useful to him, that's all.*

She had sensed a growing warmth between them, but it had all been an illusion. She had deceived herself, ignoring the warning signs that had brought her to the edge of reacting to him with dangerous intensity.

'Fool,' she muttered. 'The truth was always there before you, but you wouldn't see it. Fool!'

She lay motionless for an hour, finally drifting back into sleep. She was awoken suddenly by a noise from next door. Rising quickly, she went out into the main room, switching on the light.

'Have a heart!' said a voice.

He was there on the sofa, covering his eyes against the light.

'I'd only just gone to bed,' he complained. 'And you had to do that.'

'I'm sorry—I didn't know you were here. You weren't here an hour ago.'

'I came in quietly, so as not to wake you. I fell asleep almost instantly. It's been a heavy day.'

'Why? Has something happened?'

'In a way. Things don't always turn out the way we expect. I've had a lot of thinking to do—decisions to make.'

'Hard decisions?' she asked, as lightly as she could manage. It wasn't easy.

'Some of them.' He made a wry face, full of self-mockery. 'I'm not one of the most original thinkers in the world. I can handle business fine, but when it comes to people I tend to make a mess of it.'

'Don't be so hard on yourself. Why must you take such a gloomy view of life?'

'Is that how I seem? Well, maybe—it's just that things don't seem to work out as I hoped. I've had ideas we need to discuss before we—' He checked himself sharply, as though continuing would be a problem. 'You couldn't get me a drink, could you?'

'Tea?'

'I was thinking of something a bit stronger.'

Wine, she thought. Men always chose alcohol when they needed all their courage for a tough conversation.

She could almost hear him saying, *Ellie, I'm leaving you. I still want to see my child, but there's nothing else between us.*

How much wine would he need for that?

She poured him a glass of red, thrust it into his hand and stood waiting, silently preparing herself for the worst.

'All right,' she said at last. 'Let's hear it.'

He hesitated. 'Some things aren't easy to say.'

The words seemed to confirm her worst apprehensions.

'I'm sure you're good at them,' she said, forcing herself to speak casually.

'Sure, I've had some practice at that. More than I'd like. But we need to talk about how things

are now.' He waved his hand around the room.
'This isn't working. We're getting on each other's
nerves here, so I thought about it and—well—'

'Decided to get out,' she said quietly. Her heart
was quivering.

'Yes. That's where I've been this afternoon—
looking for somewhere. I think I've found the
perfect place.'

'When are you leaving?'

'That's up to you. I'll take you to see it later on
today. I think you'll like it, and then we'll move
in as soon as possible.'

'*We?* Did you say *we*?'

'Of course. You can't go on living here with
those rickety stairs and the lifts that don't always
work.'

She stared at him. Now her heart was thun-
dering.

'And that's what this is all about?' she whispered.

'Look, don't be offended that I went searching
without you. I wanted to see what was available.
I know what you're thinking.'

'I really don't think you do.'

'Yes, I can follow your mind by now. You believe I should have discussed it with you first,
that I take too much on myself. But I just wanted
to look at some nice places and see if any were
likely to appeal to you.'

She had been wrong. He wasn't leaving her. Her relief was so fierce that she almost lost control.

'Ellie, are you all right?'

'I'm fine—fine.'

'You don't look fine. You look as though something has knocked you sideways. I didn't mean to upset you.'

'I'm not upset. Just confused. You've been looking at apartments?'

'I've seen several, and there's one in particular that I think would be right for you. The sooner you see it the better, so why don't we go today?'

'You mean you've already made an appointment?' she guessed.

'Yes, I felt I should. Sorry about not consulting you first but I didn't want it to slip through our fingers, so I've arranged for us to see it.'

'But I have to go to work.'

'Can't you slip out for an hour at lunchtime? I don't want you to miss this.'

She didn't want to miss it either. She was alive with curiosity to see the place he had chosen as right for her.

'All right, I'll come at lunchtime.'

'It's a date. I promise you, this place will make your head spin.'

Her head was already spinning, but in ways he must not be allowed to know.

'I'll see you in the morning,' she said, and left him quickly.

Alex Dallon was waiting for her when she reached work, full of praise for her skill in looking after a wealthy client.

'I heard what Signor Fellani was saying about his English sales yesterday,' he said. 'It would be good for his business to have a branch over here. And it would certainly be good for our business to handle his profitable stuff. So try to keep him in a cheerful mood.'

'I'm having lunch with him today.'

'Good work. Take as long as you need. Call him now and tell him to collect you early.'

She did so, and was ready when Leonizio arrived at midday. Alex gave her a thumbs-up sign and waved them off.

'You're doing my career a mass of good,' she teased when they were settled in the back of a taxi. 'Alex thinks you're planning to expand into an English branch, and he's tasked me with making sure that you do.'

'Sensible man. So is that why you're with me now?'

'Officially, yes.'

'It's all going to be very interesting. But let's get this apartment sorted first.'

'Yes. I'm really looking forward to seeing it. Is it far?'

He gave her a scrap of paper on which he'd written the address, and her eyebrows rose. It was only a short distance away, which meant it was in the expensive part of town. At last they drew up outside an elegant building, and made their way inside to an apartment on the ground floor.

It was large and well furnished, with three bedrooms, plus a well-equipped bathroom and kitchen. She liked it at once, but she guessed the cost would be beyond her.

'What do you think?' he asked.

'It's lovely but I doubt if I could afford it.'

'You won't have to. I'm paying. Yes, I know what you're thinking. You reckon this is me being controlling again. But I'm doing it for practical reasons. This place is much nearer your office, so that will be easier for you.' He added wryly, 'Unless you've decided to marry me and just forgotten to mention it.'

'No, I haven't changed my mind about that.'

'So you'll continue working, and living close will be useful. But that's not my real reason for wanting you to live here. You can't stay in that dump where you're living now. You'll have an accident on those stairs any day. Here there are no stairs and you're much safer.'

'I can see that, but—'

He laid his hand on her stomach. 'You wouldn't take risks just for the pleasure of telling me to go to the devil, would you?'

He was right, she knew. Here the baby would be far safer than in her present home.

'I guess I wouldn't,' she admitted with a smile. 'All right. You win.'

He gave a grunt of ironic laughter. 'I can only guess what it cost you to say that. You can thump me if it makes you feel better.'

'I'll save that pleasure for another time. This looks like a nice place but—isn't it really too expensive?'

'You have two options. You tell Alex how successful you've been in persuading me to open a branch here. He's impressed by your skill and gives you a huge rise. Or you could just accept that I'll pay. I'll be spending some time here when I need somewhere to stay.'

'Well—' she paused, seeming to consider '—I guess I'll end up doing it your way, as usual.'

'That's what I like to hear.'

She touched his cheek. 'And you are taking good care of me—of both of us.'

'Yes. We're a family now.'

She wasn't sure how she should answer, but he saved her from having to.

'There are different kinds of families,' he said. 'We'll have to wait and see about us. Now, let's go and make sure you can rent this place.'

'Wait,' she said quickly. 'Isn't it better if you rent it?'

'But it'll be your home.'

'Not yet. Don't hurry me.'

'All right,' he said reluctantly. 'It will be mine— until you say otherwise.'

A short journey brought them to the estate agent's office that handled the arrangements. Leonizio organised everything with his usual stern efficiency and in a short time the key was his.

When they returned to the new apartment she had to admit that it would be a pleasant place to live. Leonizio showed her into the main bedroom, which contained a double bed. But he made no attempt to join her there, retreating into the second bedroom.

Ellie studied everywhere carefully, lingering in the doorway of a third smaller bedroom.

'This is just what I need,' she murmured.

'For the baby, when it's born?'

'No, for the help that I'll have to hire. I want to keep my job, which means I'll have to employ a nanny to live in and care for my child.'

'You mean our child, don't you?' he asked quietly.

'Yes, our child.'

He touched her cheek gently. 'Don't shut me out, Ellie.'

'I didn't mean to. But we won't be living together all the time.'

'We would if you married me.'

'But I can't.'

'Can't or won't?'

'It's just not a step I feel I can take, and I have to make plans for when you're not here. But I won't shut you out, I promise.'

'You *are* shutting me out.'

'I'm sorry. I wish I could do what you want but it's not so easy. There's something in me that just can't— I guess I'm just awkward.' She gave a brief laugh. 'Just like you. Well, you know that by now. But I'm not spiteful, and I want you to be happy with your child.'

She spoke warmly, and he returned her smile. The moment passed and all seemed well between them, but she could sense the tension that had briefly possessed him. It was a reminder, if she needed it, that only one thing really mattered to him. And it wasn't herself.

'Now tell me,' he said, 'do you like this place?'

'Yes, it's lovely.'

'You're not thinking of me as a controlling fiend any more?'

'I never said that.'

'Not out loud, but admit it, when we arranged to come here you were thinking the worst of me.'

'How do you know that?'

'Because you always think the worst of me. It's your default position.'

'Well, I don't like you paying for everything,' she agreed.

'Too late. You've already agreed to accept it.'

'In a sense, but I must tell you—I'm not going to give up my own apartment.'

'You what? But you don't need that place any more.'

'But I do. Please try to understand—it's mine. When I'm there I'm myself, completely myself. It's like my own little kingdom.'

'But, Ellie, we're a couple now. This will be our home.'

She clenched her hands desperately. 'No, we're not a couple. Maybe one day we will be but there's a lot we still need to know. And it's too soon to call it our home. I still need my own place.'

He gave her a look of wry bitterness. 'So that if I annoy you, you can walk out, tell me to go to blazes and escape into your kingdom. That's letting me know where I stand, isn't it?'

'It's telling you that there are still question marks hanging over us. We need to give it a little time. Please, Leonizio, don't let's argue any more. Let's just wait and see how things work out.'

Reluctantly he shrugged.

'I guess I have no choice. You win.'

'Good.' Having scored a victory, she felt her mood soften. She was going to enjoy the next few moments. 'And now I have some news for you. I'm planning something that will annoy you, but you'll just have to accept it.'

He looked uneasy. 'What's this? You're annoyed with me and you're going to make me suffer?'

She gave him a teasing smile. 'Terribly.'

'You're going to thump me, kick me in the shins, lock me in the cellar?'

'No, that would be boring. I'm planning something that you'll object to a lot more. But you have no choice. I simply won't accept a refusal.'

'You're scaring me.'

'Good. You're going to do what I say without argument.'

'I can't wait to hear this.'

'Tonight we're going out for a celebratory meal. And I shall pay for it, whatever it costs. I want no arguments. However much you dislike it, you'll just have to put up with it. *I'll* pay, not you. Do you understand that?'

His face brightened as he understood her jokey mood.

'Yes, ma'am, no, ma'am. Three bags full, ma'am.'

She burst out laughing and he joined in, wrapping his arms about her and hugging her tightly. 'I mean it,' she cried. 'Don't you dare try to pay. Don't even mention money or my revenge will be terrible. Now, let me finish settling in here, then I'll sort out the details for tonight.'

CHAPTER EIGHT

ELLIE CHOSE THE restaurant carefully. It served Italian food, luxuriously presented, and was one of the best in London. Also one of the most expensive. In this too she was making a point to Leonizio. He might have more money but she had enough to cope, and she would show him that she couldn't be bought and sold.

She called, booked the best table and gave a happy sigh of anticipation. She was really looking forward to this.

When the time came she put on the glamorous dress he'd bought her for the opera.

'Very nice,' he said, nodding approval.

'Is it?' she asked, turning around in front of a floor-length mirror. 'I shan't be able to wear it when I start putting on weight.'

'But just now it's perfect. The only thing you need to change is to let your hair hang loose.'

She let it fall, and at once her other self confronted her from the mirror.

'I'm not sure,' she said, pushing it back a little.

'Let's see.' He took over, brushing his fingers against her face until they became wreathed in hair. 'Like that? No, perhaps this way.' He drew her tresses forward again. 'I like it like this.'

'But drawn back makes me look more sensible. Which I am, although you don't want to believe it.'

'Perish the thought. I prefer the girl who seduced me.'

She gave him a teasing smile. 'Oh, yes? Are you sure who seduced who?'

He grinned. 'Well, I can't quite make up my mind. My partly conceited side tells me I was the seducer. My totally conceited side says it was you who wanted me. My hopeful side says it was mutual.'

He was still smiling as though his words were humorous. But there was something in his eyes that made her heart beat a little faster.

'I guess your hopeful side—is very knowing,' she said, a touch breathlessly.

He nodded. 'I like to think so. After all, you could always have socked me on the jaw.'

'Yes, but it wouldn't have been very polite. And I'm a polite person.'

He kissed her cheek. 'I'm glad of that. Let me get dressed and it'll be time to go.'

He vanished. Not until he was gone did Ellie yield to the temptation to touch her cheek where his lips had brushed it.

When he reappeared, dressed in elegant evening clothes, she had to admit that his conceited side had a point. He was the most attractive man she had ever seen, and his hopeful side was right. Their lovemaking had been mutual.

But she concealed these thoughts beneath an efficient manner, and they set off.

As they reached the restaurant she had the satisfaction of seeing him gape with astonishment at the luxurious place.

'Ellie, you can't mean here. You'll never be able to afford it.'

She met his eyes, her own full of teasing, to reassure him that their battle was light-hearted, although she meant every word.

'You don't know that,' she told him. 'In fact, you don't know the first thing about me, except that I've always given in and let you have your own way. Now I'm asserting myself because it's time for a change.'

'I guess it is.'

'So come along, our table is waiting.'

A waiter greeted them, checked her booking and led them to a table in an alcove by a window. There they studied the menu.

'Great food,' Leonizio observed. 'But did you really think the prices would be so high when you made me this offer?'

'It wasn't an offer, it was a command,' Ellie reminded him.

'But perhaps you'd like to have second thoughts.'

'Don't even mention it. I've made my own choice.'

She indicated two of the most expensive dishes on the menu and he followed her lead, occasionally pausing to give her a questioning glance. She met it with a smile.

'Here's the waiter,' she said. 'You give him the order for the food and wine. And mineral water for me.'

He did so, but he had a surprise for her. When it came to the drink he simply ordered mineral water for both of them.

'Did you do that for the sake of my purse?' she demanded when the waiter had gone.

'No, I did it because we're in this together. Can't you understand that?'

'Yes, I guess I can,' she said, pleased. 'All right, one up to you.'

'One up to me? That makes a change. Normally you enjoy wrong-footing me, don't you?'

'However did you guess?'

'I'm getting used to it. I'm even beginning to enjoy it.' He gave a brief laugh. 'I've got to say this for you; you're never dull.'

'So you'd like a few more threats as entertainment?'

'Why not? I'm sure you've got plenty up your sleeve.'

'You'll find out—gradually. You might find me a very interesting enemy.'

His face softened. 'Joking apart, you're not my enemy. You're my best friend. And you always will be.'

'Friend?' she echoed, instinctively touching her stomach.

'Yes, I know it sounds a little strange, considering our history. But in a way it's our success. We have a lot of arguments, but we've spent some valuable time trying to get to know each other. You said I don't know the first thing about you, but I think I know the things that matter.'

'I wonder what they are,' she mused, giving him a speculative glance. 'We might have different ideas about that.'

'We know how to make each other laugh. And, let's face it, I also know how to make you good and mad.'

'And that's important?'

'Considering how mad you can make me, I think it's vital. When I think of our future I see some of the most entertaining rows there have ever been.'

'Hmm. I wonder who'll win,' she mused.

'My money's on you. You know more of my weak spots than I know of yours.'

'Weak spots?' she echoed. 'You have weak spots?'

'Don't pretend you don't know by now. It's you who can knock me into a corner.'

'Very tactfully said, but I think it's just about even.'

'We'll have to wait and see.'

At last the meal arrived, everything was set out on the table and all was ready.

'Here's to you,' Leonizio said, raising his glass in salute.

'No, here's to us,' she said, raising her own. 'It's all going well, and we're a great success.'

He clinked glasses with her.

'I'm not sure I can claim to be a great success. You said that you always let me have my own way, but that's not true. I don't see any wedding ring on your finger.'

'Weddings aren't the only things that matter,' she hedged.

'They are if you're having a child. But let's leave it for the moment. In time you may come to feel differently. At least I hope so.' For a moment he paused, seeming to consider, as though trying to make a decision. At last he said heavily, 'I don't want to lose that special feeling you give me. It means more than I can say.'

She could hardly believe her ears. A special feeling. Had he really said that?

'Couldn't you try to say it?' she murmured.

'It's hard because I'm not sure of the right words to describe it.'

But it's called love, whispered a voice in her heart. *Why is it so hard to say?*

If only he would speak of love, then perhaps she might be able to marry him. Somewhere deep inside her was the hint of an emotion that longed to respond to him, but could never do so while he kept his distance.

'The fact is—I want to tell you about how I've felt since that first day we made love,' he said. 'You inspired me with a feeling of—' He paused again.

'A feeling of what?' she asked softly.

'A feeling of—safety.'

'"Safety"?' she echoed, only half believing.

'It goes back to that time we spent together. Do you remember it?'

How could he ask her? she thought desperately. That wonderful hour had lived in her mind ever since, never banished for long, always returning.

'Yes, I remember,' she said quietly.

'So do I. I'll never forget how it felt when we were talking and I looked into your eyes and saw there a sympathy and understanding unlike anything I'd ever known. I knew then that you were different from all other women, with a generosity and kindness that I had to reach out to, hoping it would reach out to me. And you did.

'Since that day nothing has been the same. I don't just mean because of the baby. I mean because of you, because of your strength. You're the one person I've ever met that I know I could trust with my life, and with everything that's in my life. I've been betrayed so often—'

By Harriet, she thought, who had seemed to offer him new hope, then snatched it away, leaving him desolate.

'But you make me feel that there's someone in the world who can be relied on,' he said. 'With you I know I'm safe.'

Suddenly he checked himself and spoke self-consciously. 'Oh, heavens, listen to me. Why am I talking like this? Admitting that I cling to you for safety.'

'Isn't it true?'

'Yes, it's true, but there are some things a man shouldn't admit. It's not exactly macho, is it?'

'Do you have to be macho?' she asked.

'I'm supposed to be. Ask anyone who's done business with me. Hard, cold, grim, unyielding, unforgiving. That's my reputation.'

'And with them you should keep it up. But not with me.'

'No, because I trust you as I thought I'd never trust anyone again.'

He took her hand in his and raised it to his lips.

'Thank you,' he whispered.

'I'm glad if I've given you something.'

'You've given me everything. And when our child is born you'll give me everything again. A future, a reason to live. I even think—'

He stopped suddenly, his face filled with dismay and tension. Following his gaze, Ellie saw a man and a woman entering the restaurant. The woman was young, beautiful and heavily pregnant.

'Oh, goodness…' she breathed. 'Isn't that—?'

'Yes,' Leonizio said softly. 'It's her.'

Ellie could just recognise her as Harriet, the woman in the pictures in his possession. She was filled with shock at suddenly finding her here, and Leonizio's expression told her that he felt the same.

Harriet and her companion had not noticed them, being totally absorbed in each other. Harriet's eyes were fixed adoringly on her lover's face, and his attention was riveted on the swell of her pregnancy.

Leonizio turned his head away sharply, as though unable to bear the sight.

'Is that really her?' Ellie asked.

He turned his gaze on her and she was astounded at the change in him. The gentle affection of a moment ago was gone, replaced by harsh suspicion.

'Yes, it's really her,' he said. 'You knew, didn't you?'

'What?'

'You knew they would be here. That's why you chose this place. How could you?'

She stared at him in outraged disbelief. 'You think I knew she was coming? You actually think I brought you here on purpose? How could I even know that she would be here?'

'You chose this place. Am I supposed to believe that it's coincidence?'

'Yes, because it is. I didn't know. I chose this because it's the best Italian restaurant in London. If I'd known she would be here I'd have found somewhere on the other side of town. Leonizio, you've got to trust me. I would never play such a trick on you. How could you imagine I'd ever be so spiteful?'

'I don't know. But it's enough to make a man believe in a malign fate.'

'Let's hope it teaches you not to make meaningless speeches,' she said bitterly. 'It's only a minute ago you were saying how much you trusted me. I'm telling you I didn't know she would be here, and if you can't bring yourself to believe me then your so-called trust means nothing.'

She braced herself for a vitriolic response but he didn't reply. Instead, his shoulders sagged and he sighed.

'I'm sorry,' he muttered. 'I should have known better than to blame you, but I'm in such a state, I don't know if I'm coming or going.'

'If you ever treat me like that again you'll be going. A long way away. And for ever. I won't have it, do you understand? I deserve better from you than that. Now, let's get out of here.'

'No!' His tone was quiet but forceful. 'I'm not going to run away as though I was scared of her.'

On the last words his voice faded as though something had stunned him. Following his look, Ellie saw that Harriet was holding out her hand for the man to put a ring on it.

'Their engagement,' Leonizio said bitterly. 'Now our divorce is almost finalised she's a free woman, they can marry and acknowledge that her child is his. I've played right into her hands.'

'No,' Ellie said fiercely. 'You've claimed the right to live your own life and to hell with her.' She took his face between her hands and said, 'Forget her. She doesn't exist any more.'

'You're right—you're right—'

'And we are leaving. Waiter, my bill, please.'

Leonizio made no protest, seeming content to follow her lead. In a few moments they were on their way out.

'That was a great meal,' he said. 'Thank you.'

'Yes, it was good to celebrate,' she agreed. 'Now, it's time to go home.'

'Home,' he echoed. 'That sounds nice.'

'Yes, doesn't it?' She took his hand. 'Let's go.'

Outside the restaurant there were several taxis

waiting. She hailed one and headed towards it. But suddenly her foot seemed to turn and she felt herself falling. The next moment Leonizio had seized hold of her.

'I've got you,' he said. 'Just hold onto me.'

She did so. 'I'm all right, honestly.'

'Better be on the safe side,' he said, lifting her in his arms and heading for the taxi.

As he turned to set her down she glanced over his shoulder and gasped at what she saw. There was a woman looking out at them through the restaurant's window. Her face was disconcertingly like Harriet's.

Perhaps Harriet *had* noticed Leonizio in the restaurant and tracked them as they left, curious about his companion. Now she was watching them as they clung together.

Surely not, Ellie thought.

She tried to look back again, but the face had vanished from the window. The next moment she was in the taxi.

I'm just imagining things, she thought. *At least I hope I am.* She didn't need any more complications.

They didn't speak again until they reached the apartment.

'Shall we celebrate a fine evening with another drink? Even if it's only a cup of tea?' Leonizio attempted to lift the dark mood that had descended between them.

'Thank you but I'm very tired,' she said quickly. 'I can hardly keep my eyes open.'

'Goodnight then.'

She departed for her own room, undressed and got into bed quickly, feeling a strange need to escape him. The evening's events had left her in a turmoil. Leonizio had spoken with such fervent emotion that she had been sure it was a declaration of love. The truth, when it came, had been startling.

The one time he had made love to her, it had not been out of passion but out of a need to cling to her.

She knew that many women would have entered eagerly into such a marriage, glad of a husband who needed his wife so intensely. She thought of her own mother, shut out of her husband's needs and emotions, devastated by the isolation.

But there's more than one kind of isolation, she thought. Leonizio wanted her, but not in the right way. He didn't love her and that mattered. She wished it didn't, but she couldn't deceive herself. They could never have a happy marriage.

But there was something else that tormented her. How quickly his faith in her had turned to suspicion.

One moment he was saying that he trusted her as he'd thought he would never trust anyone again. The next moment he'd accused her of playing the most appalling, spiteful trick on him.

How bitterly he'd asked, *'How could you?'*

True, he'd recovered himself at once and apologised, but she couldn't forget the burning suspicion in his eyes. Instinct told her that he'd asked her forgiveness with his brain, not his heart.

He didn't really mean that apology, she thought. He just wanted to keep her on side for the sake of their child. But that suspicion would always be there. He might think he trusted her, but at the back of his mind there would always be a doubt. And that doubt would come between them.

She kept her eyes closed, hoping to vanish into the safety of sleep. But was there anywhere that was really safe?

In his own room, Leonizio stripped off his clothes and lay down, but almost at once he rose to his feet again, knowing that it was useless trying to sleep. Tonight, things had happened that both gladdened and confused him. The moment when he'd suspected Ellie of treachery had burned into him with terrifying pain. If she could not be trusted then nothing and nobody in the world could be trusted.

He'd pulled himself together, fighting off the

sensation that the world had collapsed about him. But it had left him weakened and fearful. He needed to explore and understand his feelings, yet something warned him to keep a safe distance, lest exploring only confused him with more mysteries.

For half an hour he managed a kind of restraint, but then he couldn't stand it any more and slipped out of his room, heading for hers, two doors away.

Quietly he entered, going closer to the bed where she lay motionless, her breathing soft and steady. Slowly he dropped to one knee, leaning close to her until he could feel her breath on his face.

'Ellie,' he whispered, 'can you hear me? I hope you can. I so much need to tell you everything I feel. When I said you were my friend, and you made me feel safe, I meant that you're the most important person in the world. I thought you'd know everything I meant because we once talked about friendship and how much it matters in marriage. Do you remember that? I thought we'd understand each other at last.

'I know that's not easy. Sometimes I think we'll never understand each other. At other times I believe we'll find a way. Don't you think so?'

She didn't answer. He waited, holding his breath, while she began to twist restlessly, her arms flailing until one hand brushed his bare chest. But it fell away at once, and he knew she hadn't meant to touch him. She didn't even know he was there.

'You're not awake, are you?' he whispered, drawing back. 'You haven't heard a word I've said.' He gave a sigh. 'But, since everything I say seems to annoy you, perhaps that's just as well.'

He rose, backing out of the room, keeping his gaze on her until the last moment.

Only when she heard the door close did Ellie open her eyes. For a while she lay staring into the darkness while the sounds and sensations whirled in her.

The most important person in the world. He'd said it, but then been glad that she couldn't hear him. Hadn't he? Or had he meant—something else?

He'd said they might never understand each other. Or perhaps they might find a way.

Don't you think so? he'd asked in a voice that sounded like a plea.

But she didn't know what to think. And perhaps she never would.

Rising next morning, Ellie dressed and went out into the main room.

'Are you up?' she called.

Silence.

'Leonizio. Are you there?'

Silence.

Flinging open the door of his room, she found it empty. There was no sign of him anywhere in the apartment, and her heart sank.

He'd gone. The events of last night had disillusioned him. How quickly he'd mistrusted her. How fearful he was of life with her. Even the hope of their child wasn't enough to bring him back. The voice she'd heard in the night had been no more than a dream.

A fantasy, she told herself bitterly. *You heard what you wanted to hear because you need to believe you're growing closer. But the reality is he's gone and left you in a desert.*

But then a sound from the front door made her turn her head to see something she could hardly believe. There was Leonizio, entering with his arms filled with newspapers.

'I went out to the newsagent,' he said. 'I ordered us a delivery every morning, and bought several papers. Ellie? Ellie, are you all right?'

'Yes, I'm fine.'

'Sure? It seems that whenever we meet you look as though you've had a nasty shock. Do I have that effect? Do you want to get rid of me?'

She pulled herself together, managing to say in a teasing voice, 'Suppose I said yes. Would you vanish?'

'I might try to persuade you I'm not as terrible as you think. But I doubt I'd succeed.'

She laughed, almost dizzy with the pleasure of having him back when she'd seemed to lose him for ever.

'I'll leave you to think about that,' she said. 'Time I made the breakfast.'

Over breakfast they scanned the newspapers until she said, 'Aha! Look what I've found.' She showed him a column of text. 'If you really want a factory in England there's a building in this area that might be ideal. Apparently the owners have big financial problems.'

He studied the paper eagerly. 'So I might get it at a knock-down price. Well done! I'll get onto this today. But first I'll call Alex Dallon and tell him what a brilliant job you're doing as my right hand. Then he'll be only too glad to give you the time off.'

'You really know how to move the pieces to your own advantage, don't you?' she laughed.

'Of course. To gain control, that's what you've got to do,' he replied. 'One thing I've learned in business is that power is everything. If you're not in charge you have no control over your fate.'

'Control over fate,' she mused. 'But who in the world has that, ever?'

'We're going to have it if we do things properly.'

'Will we? Or are we hoping for too much?'

'Stop looking on the dark side, Ellie. We're going to make things happen as we want them to.'

'You make it sound so easy.'

'If you're determined enough it can be easy.'

'All right. Let's stop nattering and get out and view that building.'

'That's my girl!'

CHAPTER NINE

LATER THAT MORNING Ellie contacted the estate agent to arrange for them both to look over the building. She was about to call Leonizio when Rita, her secretary, appeared in the doorway.

'There's someone to see you,' she said. She lowered her voice to add, 'It's *her*.'

'Who is *her*?' Ellie queried, but fell silent when she saw Harriet standing behind Rita.

Now she realised that she had always known this would happen. Two women at war with each other were always bound to meet.

'Please come in, Signora Fellani,' Ellie said calmly.

Up closer, Harriet was a beautiful woman, but her face was sharp, her eyes hard.

Her pregnancy was nearing its final moments. Ellie pulled out a chair for her and Harriet edged carefully into it.

'I don't call myself Signora Fellani any more,' she said. 'I stopped being Leonizio Fellani's wife months ago, when I couldn't stand him any longer.'

'Are you saying he ill-treated you?' Ellie said, speaking with difficulty.

'That depends what you call ill-treatment. He didn't knock me about. He didn't have other women. The world would have said he was a good husband, except when you got close to him, tried to look into his heart and found that there was nothing there.'

'I really don't think—' Ellie began carefully.

'You don't think I should be telling you the truth about what a cold, hard man he is because you don't want to know it. Oh, yes, I know all about you and Leonizio. I've heard the rumours but I didn't believe them until last night when I saw you together.'

'You saw a lawyer dining with her client—'

'So I thought until I saw how you were with each other at the table. And then you ended up in his arms.'

'So it was you watching us through the window. But what you saw was an accident. I fell over.'

'Don't try to fool me. You're in love with him. I recognise the signs because I was in love with him once. It was the biggest mistake I ever made. Oh, he's pleasant enough until he gets his own way, but that's all that matters to him. And if he doesn't get it—heaven help you!'

'You didn't love him,' Ellie said passionately. 'If you did, you could never have gone with another man.'

'I found a man who truly valued me, put me first, treated me as though I mattered. You know what Leonizio cares about? His business, his ambitions, his power, *himself.* And people fall for it. They all jump to do his bidding. But you'll learn. He'll break your heart as he broke mine.'

'As you broke his,' Ellie raged.

'He's hurt because of the child, not because of me.' She leaned closer to Ellie. 'I'm really sorry for you. On the outside you're all businesslike efficiency. Who could suspect that you could let emotion get the better of you? But I think you have. You won't admit it to yourself, but it's true. And he'll make you pay for it.'

'Get out,' Ellie said furiously. 'Get out of here *now.*'

A jeering smile illuminated Harriet's face. 'Don't worry, I'm going. You've told me all I need to know.'

In the doorway she paused, looking back. 'I tried to warn you. Never forget that.'

Then she was gone.

For a moment Ellie was too shocked to move. At last she managed to make her way to the door and look out into the corridor. It was empty. There was no sign of Harriet. It was as though she had never been there, except for the legacy of dread and dismay she'd left behind in Ellie.

Businesslike efficiency. That was what Harriet

had said, and at this moment she must cling to it, doing her job, refusing to let herself be disturbed by what she had heard.

The phone rang. She snatched it up and heard Leonizio's voice.

'Did you call the estate agent?' he asked.

'Yes. He's expecting you this afternoon.'

'Can you come with me?'

'Yes, I've no appointments.'

As she'd expected, Alex was ready to give her the time off to indulge such a client. It brought back the uneasy memory of Harriet saying that people jumped to do Leonizio's bidding.

Leonizio arrived to find her waiting for him outside her office.

'Are you OK?' he asked. 'You look a bit shaken.'

'No, everything's fine.'

She wondered if she should tell him about Harriet's visit, but just now she couldn't bring herself to do it.

Together they inspected the building. It was a large, bleak-looking place that had been built nearly fifty years ago. As far as Ellie could tell it was in good condition, but she could be sure of little else.

She found it hard to know if Leonizio was pleased with what he saw. He allowed very little satisfaction to be revealed to their guide.

'It's not quite what I expected,' he observed at last.

'There's more I could show you,' the agent said in a pleading voice.

'No need. I'll take another look around before finally deciding against it. I'll see you before I go.'

When the agent had hurried away Ellie said, 'So you really don't like it?'

'Whatever gave you that idea?'

'You told him—'

'I said what was necessary to knock the price down. In fact it's ideal for me. I can see exactly where I'll put all the machinery. Let me show you.' He led her to a nearby wall. 'The toe-laster will go at this end.'

'Toe-laster?'

'It's the machine that shapes the front point of the shoes. And over there I'd put the heel-attacher, which makes sure the heel is straight with the toe. A little further on there's the perfect place for the finishing room.'

'You've got it all worked out,' she said, dazed. 'However did you do it so fast?'

'It was obvious to me the moment we came in. Not that I said so to the agent. If I'd told him how much I really like this place it would have cost me a fortune.'

'You conniving so-and-so!' she exclaimed.

'I'll take that as a compliment. It's just another name for a good businessman. I do it my way and I won't yield more than I have to.'

She looked at him with interest. 'But you don't just mean that in business, do you? That's how you live as well.'

He seemed to consider.

'Mostly,' he said at last. 'Sometimes I achieve my victory, sometimes I'm defeated.' His tone changed, became more thoughtful. 'But the thing to be really wary of is that occasionally a victory turns out to be meaningless. You think you've won everything you want, but something you hadn't anticipated undermines it. There's no way to predict in advance what it's going to be.'

'That's true,' she said quietly. 'You can make me quite nervous that way.'

He shook his head. 'Let's be clear about one thing. I don't make you anything like as nervous as you make me.'

'Oh, surely—'

'You're the one with all the power, Ellie. We both know that.'

'And you hate it, don't you? It makes you furious with me.'

'It's not that simple.' He hesitated before saying quietly, 'I have angry moments, but there are also other moments when you make me think—'

'Think what?'

'Think all sorts of things that I don't want to think, but I have to because I'm afraid they're true. And think about how I have to change myself to—'

'Hello! Are you there?'

The voice of the agent a few yards away made them both tense. Leonizio checked himself and looked away from her.

'Yes, we're here,' he called back.

Before her eyes he became his other self, confronting the agent with a wry, dismissive manner.

'This place isn't bad,' he said grudgingly. 'But it's not worth the price that's being asked.'

'It's a very fine building,' the agent protested. 'Well built, well designed, and in good condition.'

'So I should hope. But my best offer is—'

The price he named made the other man gulp then attempt an unconvincing laugh.

Ellie regarded the ensuing discussion with fascination. Leonizio had described his business self as hard and unyielding. Now she saw that it was true.

Eventually the agent telephoned the head of the company that owned the building. A sharp conversation followed, after which he hung up and told Leonizio, 'He'll call you tonight.'

'Fine. Tell him not to keep me waiting too long. Now, I'll be going.'

She thought wryly that if he was trying to win

her admiration he was succeeding. His ruthless manner might have seemed chilling, but she'd heard enough about the previous owners to know that they had brought their financial problems on themselves by bad management. Leonizio was merely proving his skill.

As they left the building she said, 'Do you think they'll give in?'

'Not a doubt. I recognise the signs.'

Of course he did, she thought. Making the other side give in came naturally to him.

But his other words haunted her. He'd spoken of having to make changes in himself. That suggested a different Leonizio, one who could be self-critical. It was a side of him she hadn't suspected, and which warmed her to him.

On the way home he said, 'I've got some investigating to do before I conclude this. Okay if I use your computer?'

'Go ahead. You need all the backup you can get. Let me know if I can help.'

When they arrived she expected him to head straight for the computer, but he picked up the phone.

'Alex? It's Leonizio. I just want to thank you for letting me have Ellie's services. She's the best. I've found the place I want to buy and she's been a great help. I'll rely on her to handle the purchase, and I hope you'll let her hang around to help me. What's that? You will? Great! You want to talk to her? Here.'

He handed over the phone and vanished.

'Ellie?' Alex sounded full of eagerness. 'Congratulations. You're doing a fantastic job. He wants you to stick with him and I've told him you can. Well done. We won't have many customers rolling in as much money as him. Bye now.'

She found Leonizio sitting at her computer, using the Internet to connect to his firm in Italy, his professional contacts and his bank accounts.

'Great,' he said at last. 'Whatever the price, I can handle it.'

He sent a few messages, then gave the thumbs-up sign. Ellie returned it in a mutual salute.

'What's that noise?' he asked, turning in the direction of the front door.

'Maybe the postman. I think something landed on the carpet.'

She was right. A letter with her name lay there. Opening it, she found a note from a friend who lived in the same building that she had left.

The postman was about to put this through your door. I stopped him so that I could send it on to your new address.

It contained a letter that made Ellie draw a sharp breath of delight. 'They want to set a date for my first pregnancy scan,' she said.

'Great. We'll go together.' He gave her a quick sideways glance. 'Unless you object.'

'Of course I don't. How can you think that?'

'I'm not usually part of your plans.'

'Nonsense. Just because I won't marry you doesn't mean I'm shutting you out. You're this baby's father, and nothing's going to change that.'

'Thank you,' he said. 'And you're right. Nothing will change that. And I'm going to be there, part of our child's life. Always. Give them a call and set the date for us to go.'

She called the hospital, but received an offer that made her hesitate.

'It could be tomorrow,' she murmured to Leonizio.

'Excellent.'

'But won't you be busy tomorrow, making all the business arrangements? That building is important.'

He shook his head. 'Not as important as this,' he said, pointing to her belly. 'Nothing in the world is as important as this.'

Joyfully, she turned back to the phone and made the arrangements.

'Ten o'clock tomorrow morning,' she told Leonizio.

He nodded, smiling in a way that touched her heart. It had a warmth and eagerness that was unlike anything she had seen in him before. He was happy, she thought. Involvement with the baby gave him a pleasure that nothing else could offer.

That evening he insisted on cooking supper for both of them.

'You shouldn't exert yourself tonight,' he said. 'I'll even do the washing-up, while you have an early night. No arguments.'

'No arguments,' she promised.

It was lovely to be so well looked after, even if she knew that she wasn't really the object of his loving concern.

He was the same next morning when he cooked breakfast and served her carefully. When it was time to leave for the hospital he took her in his arms, drawing her close for a hug.

'Look at me,' he said at last.

She looked up and found him gazing at her tenderly.

'Are you all right?' he asked.

'I'm fine, looking forward to what we're going to find out.'

'Yes, it'll be wonderful.'

He dropped his head and she felt the soft touch of his mouth against her own, lingering for the briefest possible moment.

'We're in this together,' he whispered. 'Now, let's hurry.'

She nodded and backed out of his arms, knowing that she must escape before he sensed the reaction she could barely control. Another second and she would have yielded to the temptation to return his kiss.

Perhaps it was better that she hadn't, she thought. Her own lips might have revealed too much of the reaction she could barely control.

They reached the hospital in good time and were directed to the department where scans took place. There they were greeted by the sonographer.

'It's not a long process,' she said. 'Maybe twenty minutes. I'd like you to lie down on this couch and remove all covering from your stomach.' She smiled at Leonizio. 'Are you staying with us?'

'Definitely,' he replied.

He assisted Ellie in removing some of her clothes and took her to the couch, where she lay down.

'What actually will the scan reveal?' Ellie asked.

'Several things,' the sonographer said. 'It will give us some idea of exactly how far along in the pregnancy you are and when you're likely to give birth. That's why it's called a "dating scan", because it makes it easier to plan dates. Can you remember the date of your last period?'

'Yes, but I can also tell you exactly when the pregnancy started. It was—' She gave the date of their lovemaking.

'As precise as that?' the sonographer queried.

Ellie met Leonizio's eyes. 'Yes,' she said, smiling. 'That date and no other.'

'You didn't need to tell me that,' he said softly.

'That would mean you're about twelve weeks pregnant,' said the sonographer. 'So the baby should be about five or six centimetres. Let's see.'

She began work, smoothing some gel over Ellie's stomach, then began to move a small handheld device over it. Leonizio sat beside Ellie, taking her hand in a comforting hold. She squeezed and felt him squeeze gently back.

At last a picture began to appear on a screen just above Ellie. Astounded, she saw the shape of a little head, viewed sideways.

'Is that—?' she gasped.

'That's your baby,' the sonographer agreed. 'And it seems to be the right size.'

Ellie felt Leonizio's hand tighten. She looked up, meaning to meet his eyes but his gaze was fixed on the screen. The sonographer continued moving the device over the gel and gradually more details came into view.

'You can even see some features,' Ellie murmured.

'That's a real personality coming out,' Leonizio agreed. 'Our child. *Our child.*'

'And it seems to be a very healthy child,' said the sonographer. 'All the signs are good.'

'Perfect,' Leonizio murmured.

He put his arms around Ellie and drew her close to him, looking down into her face, his eyes shining with delight.

'Thank you,' he whispered. 'Thank you with all my heart.'

'You can get dressed now,' the sonographer said.

She went to the other side of the room, leaving them alone while she put something into a computer. Tenderly Leonizio supported Ellie as she eased down from the couch, and helped her to dress.

'Do you feel all right?' he asked anxiously. 'Did you suffer at all?'

'No, I'm well. Isn't it wonderful?'

'It's the most wonderful thing that's ever happened,' he said with intensity.

Over his shoulder she saw the sonographer signalling for her to approach, but also making a slight gesture indicating that she was to come alone.

'I'll be back in a moment,' she said, and slipped away.

The sonographer greeted her with a smile,

murmuring, 'Are you completely certain when the pregnancy started?'

'Absolutely.'

'And the information from the scan confirms it. So we know when you can expect the birth. Here.' She gave Ellie a printout from the computer. 'This is a report of everything we've discovered today, and it makes cheerful reading for you and your partner.'

'I can't believe that we actually saw our baby,' she said.

'It was an excellent picture, and you can keep it. Here.'

She held up a paper for Ellie to see. It was a printout of the picture that had appeared on the screen.

'Oh, lovely!' Ellie gasped, seizing it. 'Thank you, thank you!'

She tucked it away. Showing it to Leonizio was a treat to be enjoyed later.

As they left the hospital he said, 'Let's find somewhere to celebrate.'

When they were settled in a restaurant he ordered sparkling water for them both.

'But aren't you having champagne?' she asked.

'Are you?'

'No, we agreed I couldn't drink alcohol.'

'And neither will I.'

'Thank you. That's nice of you, but I really don't mind. Have champagne if you want to.'

'But I don't want to.'

The waiter arrived with the sparkling water. Leonizio filled their glasses and raised his to her, saying, as he had often said before, 'We're in this together. Isn't that true?'

'Oh, yes.'

'Here's to our baby. Here's to the future. Here's to the best day of our lives. At least—' he checked himself '—the best day of my life. I hope you feel the same.'

'I feel wonderful but—' she sought for the right words '—I'm cautious, superstitious maybe. Just when things seem most hopeful, that's when they can often go wrong. You told me yourself that a victory can sometimes turn out to be meaningless.'

'And I have reason to know it,' he agreed wryly. 'This isn't the first pregnancy scan I've been to.'

'You went with Harriet?'

'Yes, although she tried to persuade me not to. Idiot that I was, I didn't realise that she might have a suspicious reason. But of course I wasn't part of her life any more.'

'But could she have known for certain that you weren't the father?'

'I suppose not. She must have slept with another man while she was still sleeping with me, so she must have known it was possible but she couldn't be sure. I guess she didn't want to risk me finding out at that moment. It was only later that she decided to leave me.'

'So you went to her scan. What was it like?'

His face became bitter. 'The cruel irony is that it was pretty much like today. A perfectly formed baby, the right size, everything happening as it should. It felt marvellous, both then and subsequently. But it was an illusion, and I should have known it.'

'But how could you have known it at that moment?'

'Because I knew her, the kind of person she was. I knew she told lies when it suited her, but I told myself they were only little lies about unimportant things, so it didn't matter. She'd buy an expensive dress and pretend that it had cost less than it really had, so I just shrugged. In fact, I believed what I wanted to believe.'

'The way people do when they're in love,' Ellie ventured.

'Whatever being in love means,' he grunted.

'It means what you felt about Harriet. You ignored the truth about her because you didn't want to know it.'

'Because I'm a coward who couldn't face it.'

'Love can make people weak,' she mused.

'Is that experience talking?' When she didn't

answer he said, 'I can't believe that a woman like you has never been in love.'

'A woman like me?' She gave a little laugh. 'Awkward, stubborn, recklessly stupid, opinionated—'

'Of course. Those are the things I like best about you.'

'That's lucky, because that's the only side of me you'll ever see. It tends to get in the way of the sentimental stuff.'

Without looking directly at her, he poured himself another glass of water.

'But surely there's been some sentimental stuff in your life? What about after your ex-boyfriend left you?'

'What happened with him taught me a lesson about survival, but it doesn't haunt me. Why should it?'

'If it really meant anything to you, it would never completely go away.'

Like Harriet has never really gone away from you, she thought.

Still, Leonizio was curious about her love life. What she had told him on their first night together had made it easier for him to confide in her about his wife. Her warmth and kindness had made him reach out to her, with results that once he would never have expected.

She'd implied that a man had left her because

her looks weren't up to standard, and certainly she was no conventional beauty. But she wasn't plain. There was a beauty in her face that had little to do with the shape of her features. It was the light that sometimes shone in her eyes. There was warmth in that light, also a shrewd intelligence that could make a man want to know and understand her better.

She could intrigue him, charm him, but also make him want to fight and overcome her. The one thing she never did was bore him.

He reckoned the man who'd abandoned her because she wasn't pretty enough was a fool.

He glanced up, intending to meet her eyes, but found he'd lost her attention. She was looking around her urgently.

'Is something the matter, Ellie?'

'I'm trying to find the waiter. I'd like a little snack. Ah, there he is, but he's not looking this way. I'll go and talk to him.'

She vanished before Leonizio could protest that this was his job. For a moment he sat brooding about the events of the morning. Then he noticed where she had left the large envelope that contained the details of the scan. Eagerly he reached out to open it. There was the picture of his unborn child. He studied it, remembering the other time that had seemed full of hope, until the hope died. But this hope would not die. He would cling to that belief. He raised his head, closing his eyes, withdrawing into another world where there was only himself and his determination.

On the other side of the restaurant Ellie caught up with the waiter, asked him to attend and turned back to the table.

What she saw made her pause. Leonizio was holding the baby picture, his face full of an emotion she could not understand. Was it happiness or sad remembrance? Sometimes, when he laughed and joked with her as he often did in their relationship, he seemed like a man who hadn't a care in the world. But for him laughter was a protective shield. Beneath it there was always the sadness and vulnerability that he was determined the world would never discover.

As she watched he raised his head, closing his eyes, seeming to retreat to a place where he was alone.

Ellie had sworn to protect herself against love, but in that moment her heart went out to him. She wanted to console him, reassure him that he wasn't alone, that she was there, that she would do anything for him if only it would bring him joy and confidence.

She returned to him slowly. At first he didn't seem aware of her and she sat opposite him, staying silent until he looked down.

'Are you all right?' she asked.

'I'm fine.'

'You don't look fine.'

'It's just that—when I think I'm managing all right certain thoughts come over me and catch me unprepared.' He made a wry face. 'I don't come out of this well, do I?'

'You come out looking vulnerable, the way people do when their feelings are more than they can cope with.'

He frowned ironically. 'I don't think I can agree with that. I'm a businessman. I don't have feelings.'

'You'd really like to believe that, wouldn't you? Even though you know it's not true.'

He sighed and shrugged. 'I guess you're right. You know, I could get scared at how well you understand me.'

'Nonsense. We're best friends, remember?'

He nodded. 'The best friend I'll ever have in my life. I've begun to realise that I've never talked to anyone the way I can talk to you.'

'Not even Harriet?'

'I could never be completely frank with her, certainly not about my failings. She'd have used them against me.'

'And you think I won't?'

He gave her a warm smile. 'No, you'll just laugh at them.'

'One of the great pleasures in life,' she said with a soft chuckle. 'A man you can laugh at.'

'Let's hope I don't disappoint you.'

She had a sense of delightful warmth. They were growing closer, drawing her nearer to the moment she longed for.

'I'll let you know if you do,' she said.

'So I needn't kid myself that I'm the boss.'

'Well, I might let you kid yourself, now and then.'

'I'm sure you will. We have a saying in Italy. In any relationship the man is the head. But the woman is the neck, and the neck controls the head.'

'I must remember that. It could be useful.'

'Now you've really got me scared.'

But he smiled as he said it, and again she had the sensation of being engulfed in warmth and pleasure. Every instinct told her she was where she belonged, with the man she belonged to and who belonged to her.

If only he would admit that he did.

Briefly Harriet appeared in her mind, warning her.

But Ellie shooed her away. Harriet had admitted defeat, something she herself would never do.

The waiter appeared, apologising because he could not supply the cakes she had ordered.

'Never mind, I'm happy to go home,' she said. She wanted to be alone with Leonizio.

'Me too,' he agreed. 'It's time you had a rest.'

'I don't think I need one. I'm stronger than you think.'

'Let's not take chances on that. We've already agreed that we don't know what the future holds. Come along. Home.'

CHAPTER TEN

HE TURNED OUT to be right. On the journey home Ellie began to feel a little queasy. She was glad to lie down while Leonizio sat at the computer. She needed to think of many things, for which she needed to be alone.

As she relived the afternoon in her mind certain moments stood out. The way he'd taken her in his arms, holding her close as he might have held a treasure he wanted never to lose. The warmth in his embrace and the even greater warmth in his eyes as they met hers.

We were together, she thought joyfully. *Together as we've never been before, even when we made love. Only it wasn't love that we made. There was passion, but not the feeling that now—*

She stopped, reluctant to face what lay in wait for her, although she knew now that it could no longer be avoided.

Love, she thought. *It's been there all the time but I was afraid to admit it. I want him. I want him in every way, but all he feels for me is kindness and need because of the baby. If Harriet hadn't betrayed him he'd still be with her. That night he saw her in the restaurant with the other man, it hurt him more than he could bear.*

But there was always hope. With every day they were growing closer and surely soon they would reach the moment when he reached out to her as a man to a woman? She knew from their night together that she could inflame his desire, and perhaps with a little tenderness and encouragement she could make everything else happen.

I can make him realise he's mine, she thought. *Surely I can.*

There was a click as the door opened.

'Are you all right?' he asked. 'I didn't wake you, did I?'

'No, I'm awake.'

He came in and sat on the bed.

'I thought today must have been a strain on you.'

'It was better because you were with me. You make everything better.'

'Do I really? Sometimes I think I just drive you mad.'

She smiled. 'I don't mind being driven mad, as long as it's you.'

'Nice of you.' He laid a gentle hand on her stomach. 'It's too soon to know if we have a son or a daughter.'

'Do you prefer one to the other?'

'Not really. A man wants a son that he can raise

in his own way, teach him his own ideals. But if I could have a daughter who was like her mother, with the same wicked sense of humour, the same lovely blue eyes with the hint of something mysterious behind them—I think I might prefer that.'

The emotion in his voice almost made her weep. The moment she longed for was drawing closer. He loved her, he was hers and soon he would declare it.

'You might not like it at all,' she mused. 'A daughter like that can be exasperating. That's what my father used to say.'

'He obviously didn't know how to appreciate such a daughter. But I may manage better. With you to help me.'

Her heart began to beat a little faster as her hope grew. It was happening, everything she longed for.

'Tell me,' she said softly. 'Do you think—?'

But she was interrupted by the sound of his cell phone.

'Damn!' he muttered. 'Why do people always ring at the wrong times?'

He answered the phone with a grunted, '*Sì? Sono* Leonizio.' Then he glanced up at her. 'It's my assistant in Rome. *Ciao*, Francesco.'

As he listened Ellie saw him grow still, frowning with displeasure. She could follow enough of the Italian words to know that there was a problem. Leonizio became annoyed, and he hung up suddenly.

'He's got rocks in his head,' he growled. 'A tiny difficulty with one of our customers, and he's confused. He wants me to go back fast, actually get on the next plane.'

Her heart nearly stopped. 'Oh, no, surely not?' she whispered.

'Of course not. I told him I can't even think of it, not when there are so many things here that matter.'

She knew a leap of pleasure at his refusal to leave her.

'No,' she said softly. 'You can't go back. Not now, when there's so much happening.'

'So much happening,' he repeated. 'And so much that's going to happen that we have to be ready for.'

'But we will be ready,' she said happily.

'Oh, yes, we will. How could they imagine I'd go back to Rome when I have to be here to finish buying the factory?'

'What? The factory? You mean—?'

'There's a mass of things to do, and I'm not leaving until it's all finished.'

Her head was spinning, and she could hardly believe she'd heard correctly.

'Yes, of course. The factory is a big development. We mustn't lose sight of what's important.'

She didn't know how she'd forced herself to speak so casually when her heart was thumping with disappointment. She'd convinced herself that he would stay for her sake, that he was beginning to love her, but it was only a stupid illusion.

Fool, she thought. *He's made his feelings plain enough. Just accept it. You can always marry him.*

But she knew she could never do that. Marriage would mean a life full of the aching desolation that pervaded her at this moment.

'Perhaps you should get back onto the Internet,' she said. 'Send Francesco an email with a lot of information about the business you're engaged in here. That should make him more realistic.'

'You don't know Francesco or you wouldn't talk about him being realistic.'

'No, but I do know that realism is vital,' she whispered.

'You're right. Of course it is. And I'm going to do what you said—get onto the Internet and contact Francesco with things he needs to know. Thanks for that. What would I do without my lawyer friend?'

'Hire another lawyer?' she ventured.

'No, thank you. You've got a terrific brain, and I don't want anyone else. Come on, let's get online.'

'You want me there too?'

'You're part of the firm that's handling the purchase for me. How can I manage without you?'

He led her into the next room and started the computer. Ellie's head was reeling from his words.

You've got a terrific brain. That was his idea of a compliment. She would just have to be satisfied with it.

She performed her duties with rigorous efficiency. He was grateful, hugging her warmly, declaring that he was lucky to have found her.

She managed to follow the emails he sent to Francesco, saying that he must remain in England. She drew comfort from that. He wasn't staying to be with her, as she would have wished, but it would buy her time to draw him closer to her.

She would cling to that hope. It was all she had.

After that she forced her efficient side to take over. Returning to work, she had a good meeting with Alex Dallon, who praised her skill in securing Leonizio and assigned her the task of handling his purchase.

'There's an interesting conference coming up in a few months,' he observed. 'You might like to attend with me.'

'I'm afraid not,' she said. 'I've been meaning to tell you that I'm pregnant, and I'll be on maternity leave by then.'

'Pregnant! I never suspected. Who—?'

'Leonizio.'

'So that's it. Will we be hearing wedding bells soon?'

'No.'

'You mean the wretch won't marry you?'

'Don't blame him,' she said quickly. 'I'm the wretch who won't agree to marry.'

'What? You'd turn down a man with his money? That security? Are you out of your mind?'

'No, but I'm a woman who prefers to live her own life, make her own decisions. We can do that now. This isn't the nineteenth century.'

'But surely—you could gain so much. A rich husband, an established place in the world—'

'There's more than one way to have a place in the world,' she said. 'And marrying a rich man isn't necessarily the way to do it.'

Now her work was even more concerned with Leonizio's business as she handled the purchase of the factory. He was greatly appreciative of her efforts, and often complimented her. Soon, she thought, he would speak some loving words. Just a few. And after that she could tell him that she agreed to marriage.

One night she returned home to find the apartment empty. There was a brief note from Leonizio letting her know that he was visiting some clients.

She had supper, then an early night. But there was no sleep. His unexpected absence had revived the old fears, making her recent hopes seem foolish fantasies. Restlessness grew in her. It was intolerable to be lying here, doing nothing when so much was happening that she longed to control. But the truth was that she had no control. There was the brutal fact she must face. She could do nothing while life whirled past, spinning her in directions she couldn't see or understand.

An ironic memory came back to her: Leonizio saying, 'Power is everything. If you're not in charge you're not in control of your fate.'

He'd been talking about business but she realised his words could apply to anything. From the start they had been engaged in a power game. They smiled, laughed, teased and flirted, but the underlying tension between them had always been a battle, never completely resolved.

Where will it end? she wondered. *How will it end? Or will it ever end?*

She rose and went to the window, gazing down into the street below, which was deserted. The street lamps were out and only the moonlight broke the darkness.

He could have gone anywhere in the dark, she reckoned. What was to stop him seeking the company of a woman who satisfied him more than herself? Restlessly, she paced the floor, but stopped as she saw her door opening.

'I got back half an hour ago,' he said. 'I tried to be quiet so as not to disturb you. Then I heard you moving about. I was worried about you. Are you all right?'

The relief of seeing him there was so great that she gasped. 'Yes, yes, I'm fine.'

He came further in and closed the door. 'Why aren't you getting the sleep you need? Are you worrying about anything?'

'Worrying? Well, a little. There's a lot to worry about, for both of us.'

'You won't believe this, but when I heard movements coming from in here I got a bit scared,' he said. 'I thought you might have decided to slip away from me in the night, and I could hear you getting ready to go.'

'That's funny,' she said. 'I thought you'd vanished too.'

'Don't be silly. The only thing that bothers me is the thought of losing you. I'd do anything to prevent that.' His voice became gently humorous. 'Lock you up, bolt the door, bar the windows.'

'In other words, keep me a prisoner?' she asked lightly.

'I'll do what I have to.' He wrapped his arms

about her. 'Don't forget I'm ruthless in pursuit of my ends.'

She rested her head against him. 'So am I,' she said.

His arms tightened a little. 'You might be shocked to know just how terrible I can be.'

'I could say the same.'

'Are you warning me to beware of you?'

She raised her head to look him in the eye.

'You already know that,' she whispered.

'I guess I do. But it might be interesting to find out the rest.'

He drew her closer, letting his mouth rest on hers in a way that made her heart beat faster. But suddenly he tensed and drew away.

'I'm sorry,' he said. 'I should have more self-restraint.'

'You mean you shouldn't kiss me?'

'If we went any further I couldn't stop at kissing you. I want to make love to you but—well, I know I mustn't. Not now.'

'Leonizio—'

'When our child is born and it's safe again, then we'll make love urgently. We'll have a wonderful night. But now I could do harm to you and the baby. I'm just concerned for you both.'

No, she thought. *You're concerned for the child. Not me.* Besides, it simply wasn't true that making love would hurt their baby. The medical advice she'd received had reassured her that there was no danger of that at all. But it hurt that Leonizio seemed to be using her pregnancy as an excuse to keep her at arm's length.

She was still tormented by the flood of desire that had risen in her, and which now turned into agonising emotion. She tried to control it but it overcame her and suddenly she began to cry. Tears poured down her face, defeating her efforts to stop.

'Ellie, please—'

'Go away,' she choked.

'I'm sorry I made you cry. I should have remembered that it happens easily in pregnancy. Harriet used to cry over nothing at all.'

'Yes, and you didn't care for her feelings.'

'Don't say that. How could you possibly know?'

'Because she told me what you were like.'

She spoke without thinking, and knew at once that she had done something disastrous. Leonizio's hand on her shoulder grew tense and his voice was harsh.

'What did you say? Have you and Harriet been talking?' His hands gripped her painfully. 'You told me you and she weren't in cahoots, but you were lying, weren't you?'

'No, I wasn't. She turned up in my office the other day. I didn't invite her and I threw her out.'

'But that night in the restaurant—'

'I hadn't met her then. I didn't meet her until she arrived in my office. She saw us together and wanted to come prying. She said things about you that I couldn't bear.'

'What did she say about me? Tell me.'

'I didn't mean to talk to her—'

'Tell me!'

'She said she wanted to warn me that you were a hard man with an empty heart; pleasant enough until you got your own way, but that was all you cared about. She said everyone jumped to do your bidding, and you'd break my heart as you broke hers.'

'And you believed that nonsense?' Leonizio exploded. 'I never broke her heart. If anything, it was the other way round. But you know that. I've told you things I'd die before telling anyone else.' He broke off and a frozen look came over his face. 'Now I'm beginning to wish I'd died before I told you. You swore I could trust you.'

'But you can,' she said desperately. 'I told you I didn't know Harriet was going to be in the restaurant that night and it was true. But she saw us there and came to find me at work. I couldn't stop her, and I told you I threw her out.'

'But not before you'd put your heads together and had a sneering talk about me.'

'Why do you find it so easy to believe the worst of me?' she demanded furiously. 'Or is it just that you believe the worst of everyone?'

'I don't want to. I guess sometimes I can't help it. After all, you might have told me she'd met you before this, but you chose not to. Am I supposed to trust you after that? Sometimes the worst is true.'

'Yes, I suppose it is,' she agreed quietly. 'That's something we have to decide. I think I'll go to bed now. No, don't come with me. I want to be alone.'

He didn't try to dissuade her, but stared blankly until she had left the room. Then he turned and left the apartment, slamming the door violently behind him.

Ellie heard the slam, feeling the sound go through her. It was like listening to the world end. Whatever she had hoped might happen between them, it wouldn't happen now.

Maybe they never had a chance, right from the start. Perhaps she should have told him about meeting Harriet but she'd thought she was doing the right thing. Sometimes the right thing was the wrong thing. But it had proved that they could never have a life together.

She lay down and tried to sleep. But sleep wouldn't come. There was something she had to do. She got to work.

* * *

Leonizio returned hours later to find Ellie sitting at the computer. She rose to confront him.

'Look, we have to talk,' he said.

'I don't think so. Everything's been said and we understand each other.'

'But earlier I said things I didn't mean—'

'I know what you meant. I understand far more than you think. Now, I have something to say to you.'

He was very pale. 'What is it?'

'I've been reading Francesco's emails. I don't understand the Italian perfectly, but I can follow enough to understand that he needs you out there urgently. I think you should go.'

Silence. Leonizio looked at her closely, as though trying to read in her face the things she refused to say.

'I've told him how to handle the situation,' he said. 'If I advise him some more I'm sure he can manage.'

'No, I think you should go back there at once. Francesco obviously feels he needs you.'

'Yes, but—don't you need me to look after you?'

'Thank you but I can look after myself.'

'In some things, yes, but—'

'I don't work too hard, take too much exercise, eat the wrong food.'

'Yes, the practical things, but is everything practical? Haven't there been nights when you awoke from bad dreams and came into my arms for me to comfort you?'

Yes, she thought bitterly. *But that was a mistake, and one I regret.*

'Don't you care about things we share?' he asked.

'I care about a lot of things you never even think of,' she said.

'That's not my fault. I don't know what it's like for you to be pregnant, and what you could be going through. I try to imagine, but I'm sure I get it wrong. You should tell me more about it. Can you feel the baby moving? That sort of thing.'

'No, not yet.'

'But when you do, won't it be a wonderful moment for us to share?'

'Of course, but—there are lots of things we can't predict. It might not happen until you come back from Rome.'

'So you really think I should go?'

'Your business needs you. Don't leave Francesco fumbling on his own.' She managed to put a teasing note in her voice. 'After all, what kind of father lets himself go bankrupt?'

'Well, I suppose if you put it like that—'

'We can stay in touch.'

'Of course. We must.'

'I'll continue handling the factory purchase according to your instructions.'

'Oh, yes—I see.'

His expression showed that he'd finally understood that she was putting a distance between them.

'I guess I'd better go then,' he said.

His voice was blank and emotionless. Try as she might, there was no way she could be sure what he was thinking and feeling. And that was how he wanted it, she realised.

He telephoned Francesco for half an hour, then hung up to say he would leave that afternoon.

'It sounds serious,' he said in a low voice.

'Then you'll be gone for some time.'

'I guess so. I'd better start packing.'

She accompanied him to the airport, waiting in silent patience while he went through the formalities. For the last few minutes they went to a small café.

'Let me know when you arrive safely,' she said.

'Yes. And we must stay in touch. Let me know when you have appointments, and what the doctors tell you.'

'Of course I will.'

'How are you feeling now?'

She pointed down to her stomach.

'All is well,' she said. 'We're fine, both of us.'

He looked closely. 'You're just beginning to show a slight bump.'

'Is it really beginning to show? Oh, good! It makes everything more real, especially now I have that picture.'

'Yes, there's a new person on the way,' he said softly. 'Something to look forward to.'

Before she could reply, the loudspeaker proclaimed the start of boarding.

'Time to say goodbye,' Leonizio said. He laid his hand gently on her bump. 'Goodbye to you too, little one.'

'Goodbye, Daddy,' Ellie said.

He grinned. 'Thanks. That's lovely.' Laying a hand on her shoulder, he drew her forward and laid his lips on hers. It wasn't a passionate kiss, but it was affectionate and she returned it with pleasure.

She went with him as far as the check-in gate.

'Here's to the next meeting,' he said. 'Whenever it is.'

'I guess that's not in our control,' she said. 'We'll just have to hope for a kindly fate.'

He made a wry face. 'Don't count on fate being kind. It's more likely to be spiteful. The best fate is the one we make for ourselves. I wish—'

He hesitated, as though uncertain what to say next.

'What?' she asked.

'I wish—it's hard to explain, but I wish—if only we—'

Final call for Flight—

The crowd was moving about them, making further talk impossible.

'Goodbye,' she said.

'Goodbye—goodbye.'

She kept her eyes on him until the last moment. She had a feeling that he'd turned back for a last look at her but with so many people milling around him it was hard to be sure.

Then he was gone.

CHAPTER ELEVEN

ELLIE KNEW THAT the sensible thing would be to return home at once, but these days she found it hard to be sensible. Instead she lingered in the airport, seeking a place where she might be able to see his plane begin to move slowly towards the take-off point

As she went out to the taxi rank she heard a sound overhead and looked up to see the plane soaring into the sky. She watched until it vanished into the clouds. Then she turned away and walked back to the taxi rank.

She could sense herself moving like a robot, and even thinking like one. Leonizio was gone. Life was over. Why was she bothering to return home? What was home? Did she have any such place?

At the end of the day he emailed her to say that he'd arrived safely. She already knew, having checked the plane's arrival online. But she was glad to hear from him, even though his tone was efficient and unemotional.

But perhaps that was only to be expected, she thought. She had urged him to leave, making it plain that he was no longer welcome. And now that he had gone there was no indication when she would see him again. Or if she would ever see him again.

She returned to work at the office, seeking comfort in her career, which was reaching a high point. Alex was proud of her, assigned more cases to her care and expressed his pleasure at the way she dealt with them.

Her thoughts of Leonizio grew more confused every day. He had turned against her in a way that seemed to freeze her out. But, to her amazement, she discovered that he had taken practical steps to protect her.

Two days after his departure she received a letter from the bank saying that every month a large sum of money was to be deposited into her account, from Leonizio.

She emailed him.

Why didn't you tell me?

He emailed back.

Why are you surprised? It's my job to look after both of you.

She surveyed the words with bitter irony. In her job she often talked to mothers frantically fending for themselves because the men who'd fathered their children had abandoned them, ignoring their responsibilities.

How those women would have envied her, thinking her lucky to have a man who attended so rigorously to his financial duties.

Lucky, she thought. *That's what they'd say I am. If only they knew.*

As promised, Leonizio stayed in touch. His business dealings were troublesome, but he seemed able to get control. At her end the formalities of the factory purchase were also going well.

In this way time passed. Any hope she might have had that he would seize the first chance to hurry back proved empty. Often she relived the moment at the airport when he had said, 'I wish—it's hard to explain, but I wish—if only we—'

What had he wished? What was the meaning of 'if only'? She longed to understand but she could gain no whisper of hope.

Many times she asked herself why she had not simply taken the easy option of marrying him and enjoying whatever closeness could unite them. But she knew she couldn't have done it. The pain would have been too great. She could never have deceived herself that he loved her. If she'd had any hope his casual acceptance of their parting would have forced her to face the truth.

Gradually the time passed, more time than she had ever imagined when she'd first urged him to go. At last came something she had longed for and dreaded equally: the feeling of her baby moving in the womb.

It was what Leonizio had wanted. 'A wonderful moment for us to share', he'd said. But he wasn't here to share it. And that was her fault, she reflected sadly. She had sent him away.

She emailed him.

The baby's moving. I can feel it.

It took two days for him to reply.

Sorry to be so long but I've had to be away for a few days dealing with someone who's trying to ruin my business. Dealt with him, but got behind with my mail. Wonderful news about the baby moving. Glad everything's going well. Take care of yourself.

She was lucky enough to feel well most of the time; the morning sickness had abated now, and so she was able to bury herself in work. Alex was pleased with her success and she could sense her career climbing as never before. How she was going to combine it with motherhood was something she still hadn't worked out. But she had no doubt it could be done.

Often she would brood over the different

choices that faced her. It was hard to sort them out when she didn't know how large a part Leonizio would be playing. But she didn't regret her decision not to marry him. She was her own woman, independent, able to stand alone whatever happened. And she wasn't going to let that change.

Days passed relentlessly. Her pregnancy was now nearly twenty-four weeks along and it was time for another scan. The first one had shown everything was normal, which was likely to be the case with this one. She was in a confident mood as she entered the hospital and headed for the department.

The sonographer was the same one who had scanned her before. She greeted her cheerfully, indicating the couch. Ellie settled herself on it, then pushed down her skirt to her hips and raised her top high up, leaving a bare space for the scan.

They started work. Again the sonographer adjusted the screen in a position where they could both see it easily. She spread gel over Ellie's stomach, then began to move a handheld device over it. As before, the baby appeared on the screen.

Ellie drew in her breath in delight at the picture, larger than before. There was her child. Its head was at a slight angle, but her impression was that it was facing her, sending a silent message of love and need.

If only Leonizio could have been here now to

see this new picture. How happy it would have made him. She smiled at the picture, sending back her own message of love.

'Isn't he gorgeous?' she breathed. 'Or she.'

'One moment,' the sonographer said. 'I need another look.'

After a few more tense moments she said, 'I'm afraid we'll have to do another scan soon. The baby is a little smaller than I'd expect at twenty-four weeks. It might not be serious, but we need to discover a little more.'

'Discover what?' Ellie asked in a shaking voice. 'What will you be looking for?'

'It's too soon to say—'

'But what could the worst be? Tell me. I must know.'

'There is the possibility of foetal abnormalities. It's not certain, but there's just a chance that we have to look into.'

'Abnormalities. Oh, heavens.'

The sonographer uttered more comforting words but Ellie barely heard them. The word 'abnormalities' thundered in her head. Filled with confusion, she left the building and made her way home in a daze.

Once safely shut inside, she found a silence that descended on her like thunder. Everything she had believed in, hoped for, was suddenly snatched away, leaving her in a nightmarish desert.

For hours she remained there, sometimes walking about from room to room, sometimes sitting with deadly stillness.

At last she knew what she must do. There was only one person she could tell about this disaster. He had a right to know and he was the only person she could trust to understand. She checked the time. It was late afternoon but she might just catch Leonizio at work. She seized the phone and dialled the number of his office. The call was answered by his secretary, who fortunately spoke English.

'I'm sorry, Signor Fellani is not here,' she said.

'Where is he? I must speak to him. It's desperately important.'

'He isn't in this country. He had to go to Paris to attend a business conference. There is much depending on it.'

'When will he be back?'

'Maybe next week.'

'Oh, heavens!' she whispered through the tears that were beginning to choke her. 'Ask him to call me then. Goodbye.'

She slammed down the phone, then dived into her diary, seeking his cell phone number. Wherever he was, she would find him now. But when she had dialled she received only a recorded message saying that the number was unobtainable. She fired off an email, not giving details but urging him to call her as soon as possible. Surely he would be checking his email, even if he was away from Rome and his office at the factory?

With all her heart she longed to reach out to Leonizio, but now she felt it was hopeless. It was surely not a coincidence that she couldn't reach him. He'd switched off his cell phone and instructed his employees to shut her out.

Bitterly, she reckoned that she had only herself to blame. She had banished him from her life, and he'd accepted her decision. She couldn't hope that he would call her.

He didn't. Hours passed, darkness descended and there was no sound from the phone. She knew she was clinging to false hope. Even if he finally called, would things be any better? He valued her only because of the baby, and would he still value their child when he learned of the disaster that threatened them?

There was no escape from the despair that had descended on her. There was only desert loneliness, and perhaps that was all there would be for the rest of her life.

Suddenly the silence was broken by the sound of the doorbell, ringing urgently. She stumbled out of bed, made her way to the door and pulled it open, too dazed even to put on the light. She could barely even see who was there until she felt herself seized in his arms.

'Ellie—Ellie—'

'Leonizio—it's you?'

But it couldn't be him, said a voice inside her. Dreams didn't come true like that.

'Yes, it's me—I'm here—hold onto me.'

She did so, clinging to him frantically, desperate to believe this was really happening.

'Leonizio! But you're in Paris.'

'I was, but when I got your message I came at once.'

'Your business conference—she said there was much depending on it.'

'To hell with that. Do you think it matters beside you? What's happened?'

'Oh, Leonizio—'

'Ellie, what is it? Why did you call? What's happened?'

Suddenly tears overwhelmed her and she collapsed against him. He lifted her, carried her to the bed and sat down, still holding her.

'Tell me,' he said.

'It's the baby—there's something not right. I had another scan today and there might be abnormalities.'

'What do they mean by that? What kind of abnormalities?'

'They don't know yet. They still have to find out. They say they can't be certain. It might still be all right or…or maybe not.'

His arms tightened about her and she felt him draw her down so that they were both lying on the bed.

'Hold onto me,' he said.

'Oh, thank heavens you're here.'

'I've always been here for you, even if you didn't know it. And I always will be.'

She clutched him, burying her face against his shoulder while her tears flowed. He held her in silence, letting her weep while she needed to. He waited until she'd calmed down a little before speaking.

'Try to talk. Try to tell me everything that happened today.'

In a shaking voice she described the scan, the results.

'They'll need to do more tests,' she said, 'to find out how bad it is.'

'Of course. I have to see the medical report about the test you had today. So that I can show it to the doctors in Rome when we go over there for the tests.'

'Rome? You mean—?'

'Trust me, Ellie. I'm going to keep you with me all the time. If a disaster happens I'll be there, on the spot, to care for you.

'If you knew what my journey here was like today, terrified what might have happened, whether I'd find you alive... I can't endure another separation, so—' He hesitated before saying with a touch of nervousness, 'You have to come home with me, because I couldn't stand anything else. I'm sorry if you don't want to—'

'Yes—yes—I do want to.'

'You're sure? I know I'm giving you orders and that annoys you but—'

'You can give me all the orders you like. We're a family, all three of us.'

'Are we?' he asked. 'Do you mean that? I've never been sure that you actually felt that way.'

'But I do. You were right. There's nobody I need as much as you. *We're in this together*.'

'Yes,' he breathed joyfully. *'Yes, we are!'*

He lay down beside her. 'Go to sleep,' he whispered. 'We'll worry about the rest tomorrow. Tonight, it only matters that we're together.'

He couldn't have said anything more true. He was here. He had put her first. It was like a dream come true. She lay in his arms, holding him with love and tenderness, while some of his words echoed in her brain.

He had said, 'You have to come home with me.'

Home. Wherever he was, that was home. And never had it been truer than now.

She awoke in the dawn to find herself still in his arms. He was regarding her tenderly. He looked down at her bulge, now much bigger, and touched it with tentative fingers. His eyes were alight with pride.

'It's about time you two reconnected,' she said. 'It's been a long time.'

'Yes, too long. The way you told me to go—I had a feeling you might be throwing me out for good.'

'I could never do that. But it seemed—we've never really understood each other.'

'That's true. But the time is coming when everything is going to be different.' He looked a little anxious. 'Don't you feel that?'

'Yes, I do. But we don't know how—'

'Hush!' He kissed her forehead. 'We must make it the right way, for the sake of—' He touched her bump. 'Come now. We have much to do.'

He helped her up, and remained at her service while she dressed. Over breakfast he studied the scan report. She watched his face, frowning, troubled, but then smiling as he glanced up at her, as though determined not to worry her.

At last he returned it to her, saying, 'The sooner we're gone the better. I've checked the times of the trains.'

'We're going by train?'

'It's better that way. I know flying in pregnancy is mostly safe, but if there are any fears about the baby it's better not to fly. It'll be a long journey, but I'll make sure you're comfortable all the way.'

He took her to the station and helped her into the first class carriage he'd booked for them both. At last they started the journey from London to the coast, through the tunnel beneath the sea and on their way to Paris. There they had to change trains for the final part of the journey to Rome.

She had an uneasy journey. For much of the way she felt queasy and had a headache. Leonizio cared for her every moment and when night came and she fell asleep she awoke to find him leaning anxiously over her.

'We're nearly there,' he said. 'Did you sleep well?'

'Oh, yes,' she whispered.

She'd had a lovely night, safe and contented in the feeling that she was going home. She reached up to him and they held each other close as the train headed for the last lap to Rome.

Ellie was only vaguely aware of the next few hours. A taxi was waiting for them at the station, and soon they were on their way home.

A doctor called the same evening. He talked to her at length and studied the information from the scans.

'I will make a referral. He's the best obstetrician there is.'

He arranged the appointment for the very next

morning. Leonizio accompanied her and sat in tense silence while more tests were made.

'Is the baby really too small?' Ellie asked nervously.

'A little smaller than I'd expect, but it isn't necessarily serious.'

'But when will we know if there are any abnormalities?'

'When we get the test results. Don't assume the worst. Things could still go well.'

'And if they don't?' she wept. 'How badly could our child be hurt?'

'It's much too soon to say.'

'Could it be my fault? Have I done something wrong?'

'Stop it,' Leonizio told her. 'Don't look for reasons to blame yourself.'

'I'm afraid it's what mothers tend to do,' the doctor said. 'But sometimes things just happen for no apparent reason. I'll be in touch as soon as we know more.'

'Don't you have any idea now?' Ellie begged.

'I couldn't possibly speculate.'

His words seemed to threaten the worst. She dropped her head, feeling as though the world was crashing around her. Only the support of Leonizio's arms prevented her from crying out in despair. While he held her she could feel safe.

'Come along,' he murmured. 'Let's go home.'

They were silent on the journey home. When they reached the apartment he made her some coffee and sat beside her, sad and serious.

'I want you to stay here now,' he said. 'I have to look after you. I couldn't bear it any other way.'

'Nor could I,' she said. 'As long as we have you—'

'You do have me. Both of you.'

For the next few days Ellie tried to think as little as possible. She functioned mechanically, fulfilled her domestic duties, and did whatever Leonizio asked. But she kept her brain silent as much as possible. Brooding about what might be about to happen only brought pain.

She sensed that Leonizio was going through exactly the same thing. They didn't talk about it, but his fear was in his eyes. Whenever the phone rang he would answer it tensely, always expecting the crucial news. But it didn't come, and when he'd hung up he would shake his head and pat her on the shoulder.

At last, after three tense, agonising days, it happened.

The phone rang again. Ellie's eyes were fixed on Leonizio's face as he snatched up the receiver, grating, *'Si?'* in a harsh voice.

Then he didn't speak for several seconds, while her heart thumped with fear. But suddenly his face brightened, his eyes lit up and he made her a thumbs-up gesture.

'Yes!' he cried. *'Yes, yes!'*

He slammed down the phone and seized her in his arms.

'Good news!' he yelled. 'Everything's fine.'

'You mean the baby—?'

'Our baby is perfectly healthy. The tests say there's nothing wrong.'

'Oh, thank heavens!' She burst into sobs against him and for several moments they clung tightly, as if protecting each other from the world.

She could feel him shaking. Looking up, she saw that his face was as wet as her own, as though he too had been weeping tears of joy.

'I don't dare believe it,' she said. 'Can it really be true?'

'We're going to see them tomorrow,' he said huskily. 'And they'll show us everything. That call was just to alert us in advance.'

They saw the doctor next day and received a mass of communication that eased their minds. Also included was the estimated date of the birth, over three months ahead.

'And until then I strongly advise you to avoid all stress,' the doctor said. 'You've been lucky so far, but you're to take no chances.'

'We're going back to England,' Leonizio said.

'That's all right, as long as you go by train. No stress.'

'She'll be resting from now on,' Leonizio said. 'I'll see to that.'

'That's good to know. It's a relief to be able to leave her in your care.'

When they were alone Leonizio said, 'Aren't you going to say it?'

'Say what?'

'How dare I make decisions without consulting you? How dare I say that I'll make sure you rest when you have a job to go back to?'

She gave him a warm smile. 'I guess I know you too well by now to say any of that. I guess you've made all my decisions.'

He eyed her with a wry smile. 'Am I allowed to make your decisions?'

'I suppose I'll have to give you my permission. So tell me what I'm going to do.'

'We're returning to England because I think you'll feel happier there, and feeling happy will make you safer. You've done a great job buying the new factory, and I'm going to base myself there until our child is born.

'We settle back into our apartment and you stay there, where I can protect you and our baby, because nothing else matters but your safety.' A sudden thought seemed to trouble him. 'You did really give me your permission, didn't you? I didn't imagine that?'

'Don't worry. I'm not going to fight you about this.'

'What will Alex Dallon say when we tell him you're taking a long maternity leave?'

'He'll understand. I know it's what I must do.'

'Then everything's going well and we can stop worrying.'

'Hush, don't talk like that,' she said, urgently putting her fingers over his mouth. 'Never be too sure that things are going well. It's bad luck.'

'All right, I'll be cautious.' He gave a small wry laugh. 'I used to think that we made our own luck, that control was important. But now it's you who makes my luck, and I lost control a while back.'

'Are you saying that I have control?' she teased. 'You don't really mean that. Tomorrow you'll say just the opposite.'

'You have some control. But our little unborn friend has most of it. Since the day we knew about him he's given the orders and somehow I find myself dancing attendance.'

'He? You want a son?'

'No, I'll be happy with a girl or a boy, as long as it's mine.'

'I've promised you it's yours. Don't you believe me?'

'Yes, I believe you. When I said "mine" I didn't mean like that. I meant that he or she will call me Daddy, ask me questions, tell me what they're thinking and hoping for, give me birthday and Christmas cards. If they get into trouble I want to be the one they send for. I want to know that nothing can ever take me out of their life.'

The emotion in his voice affected her painfully. His child meant everything to him. More than she ever would.

'You can be sure of that,' she said, speaking with difficulty. 'I won't come between you.'

'Does that mean you'll marry me?'

'Don't. I can't talk about that now.'

'But why—?'

'You don't understand. There are so many things we have to—let's talk later. I'm carrying your baby. Can't that be enough for the moment?'

'Except that you could run out on me whenever you like.'

'And you think if I was your wife I'd be your prisoner? Marriage certificates and formalities don't make it work,' she persisted. '*We* have to make it work.'

'And you don't think we can? All right, don't answer that. Your refusal is an answer in itself. Let it go. I promise not to trouble you again.'

So that was it. He'd bowed to her wishes and would no longer annoy her with marriage proposals. She guessed she should feel satisfied and triumphant.

But she only felt sad and defeated.

CHAPTER TWELVE

THE TRAIN JOURNEY back to England was peaceful, and life settled down quietly. As the weeks passed Leonizio behaved perfectly. He cared for Ellie like a dutiful protective father, anticipating her needs, ensuring that she was never under strain. And, true to his promise, he never uttered a word about marriage.

Ellie supposed she should be glad of that. It made her life easier and more relaxed. And if she occasionally had moments of desolation she told herself firmly to ignore them.

Gradually she grew bigger. The time was coming when they would know everything about the future. One night Leonizio helped her undress for bed. As her bump came into view he touched it reverently.

'I'm a lucky man,' he said. 'So much happiness now, and so much more in store for us. I can hardly wait. Do we really have to wait another month?'

'So the doctors say. But it moves so much I get the feeling of a real personality in there, almost as though our child was with us already.'

'In a way it is. Hey there!' he addressed her stomach. 'Be careful of your *mamma*. Don't give her a hard time.'

'I can always hope he or she will listen to you,' Ellie chuckled. 'But I don't think I can count on it.'

'True.' He grinned, saying, 'After all, its mother never listens to me.'

'Well, that might change—ah!' She checked herself with a gasp as a sharp pain attacked her stomach.

'What is it?' Leonizio demanded. 'Ellie, what's the matter?'

'I'm not sure. I just—something happened—' She clasped her bump and gasped again.

'Is it starting?' he asked in an alarmed voice.

'It's too soon for that but—yes, I think it is. Oh, heavens, I can feel such—*ah!*'

Now there could be no mistake. The pain that went through her was fierce and threatening.

'It's happening,' she groaned.

'Happening?' he echoed in alarm. 'You mean the baby—?'

'Yes, but—oh, no—please, this mustn't happen. It's too soon.'

'I'll call the ambulance,' Leonizio said through gritted teeth.

He seized the phone, made a tense call, then gathered her in his arms.

'Hold on to me. It's going to be all right.'

Desperately she clung to him as the pain ripped through her again, warning her of possible tragedy to come. The birth wasn't due for another month, yet now—

'It can't happen yet,' she groaned. 'It can't, it can't.'

But it could. In the despairing depths of her heart she knew that fate could be against them, snatching their child away in the last few moments before life began.

Her heart broke for Leonizio. She had promised him so much, longed so fiercely to make him happy. But in a few cruel minutes it might all be snatched from him again, banishing him back into the same bleak desert from which she had vowed to rescue him.

'They'll be here soon,' he said. 'We'll go to the hospital and they'll make everything right.'

But he sounded too firm, too determined, as though he was trying to convince himself as well as her. Looking at his face, she saw fear as well as hope.

'I'll do everything I can,' she choked. 'Truly— I'll try—I'll try—I don't know why this is happening—'

'It's not your fault,' he said fiercely. 'Don't even think like that.'

They clung together until the sound of the doorbell made him go and look out of the window.

'They're here,' he said, and hurried away.

A few moments later a stretcher was wheeled into the room. Leonizio lifted her in his arms, laying her gently upon it then taking her hand, which he held for the whole journey.

She was only vaguely aware of what was happening around her. There was the hum of the vehicle, and she could hear voices as Leonizio asked fearful questions, but she could understand little. The greater reality was the surge of pain that went through her again and again.

The ambulance stopped. They had reached the hospital. Through her spinning senses she could feel herself being wheeled inside. Faces appeared, full of concern. Hands touched her gently. She heard Leonizio talking to the doctor, explaining what had happened, exactly when the pain had started.

'The baby isn't due for another month,' he said. 'That's what we were told. It can't be coming now, can it?'

'We'll have to see,' the doctor said quietly.

Again pain flooded her, making her scream. 'Leonizio—*Leonizio.*'

Hardly aware of what she was doing, she reached out blindly and felt him take hold of her hands.

'I'm here, *cara*,' he vowed.

'Don't leave me.'

'It's all right if I stay, isn't it?' he demanded of the doctor. 'I can't leave her.'

'If she needs you it may be best for you to stay,' the doctor agreed. 'But please—'

'I won't interfere or get in your way,' Leonizio promised at once.

'Excellent.'

Again Ellie cried out. Now there could be no more doubt. Her body was possessed by contractions that told her things were moving fast. She clung fiercely to Leonizio, looking up so that her eyes met his.

'Soon,' he whispered. 'Soon we will have everything.'

If only, he thought desperately, her suffering could end now. It tortured him to see her terrible pain and know that he couldn't help her bear it.

Useless, he thought. *That's all I am. Useless!*

Time passed slowly. Sometimes she seemed able to relax, but then another contraction would seize her, leaving her seemingly exhausted.

'How long can this go on?' Leonizio asked wretchedly.

'It's coming,' said the doctor. 'Any moment now—'

Then he was reaching forward to help the baby out into the world. Leonizio had a slight vision of a tiny body, but it did not seem to move and he held his breath, silently praying in hope.

Suddenly it happened. The air was split by a wail that grew in vigour until everyone was smiling with relief.

'That's it,' exclaimed the doctor in delight. He examined the baby closely. 'It's a girl. She's a little small and she'll need extra care at first, but the signs are good.'

Leonizio leaned close to Ellie. 'Did you hear that, *carissima*? We have a daughter, and we're a family. Isn't that wonderful?'

But her eyes stayed closed and she only murmured, 'Mmm?'

'Ellie—Ellie—'

'I'm sorry but you'll have to leave now,' the doctor said grimly. 'She's losing a lot of blood and it needs urgent action.'

'Or what?' he demanded. 'If she loses too much blood—what will happen?'

'Then we'll have a tragedy, which we're fighting to prevent. Please, you must go now.'

Leonizio felt like tearing his hair out. He knew he must go but he couldn't bear to leave Ellie. Her eyes were still closed and he didn't know how much she heard. Leaning down, he kissed her forehead, her cheeks, her mouth.

'I'll be back,' he whispered. 'Just promise to be here, waiting for me.'

He went out into the corridor and found a seat just a short distance from the door. From here he could return in a moment if she needed him.

But he couldn't banish the thought that she didn't need him and would never need him again. She was disappearing into another world.

He had the strangest sensation of watching a parade. Everyone he had ever cared about was there, reminding him how little warmth and love there had been in his life and how cruelly it had vanished. The uncle and aunt who had raised him had merely done their duty, without giving him anything he could feel as affection. With Harriet there had been love, or so he'd thought until she'd betrayed him. And the child he'd believed his, who'd inspired his love while still in the womb. That love too had been snatched from him, abandoning him in what would have been a desert but for Ellie.

With Ellie there had finally been hope, but now she too was slipping away, leaving him the baby he wanted so much, but which he now realised could never console him for her loss.

He tensed as the door to the delivery room opened and a nurse emerged pushing a small trolley. She came over to him.

'I'm taking your daughter to the Special Care Unit,' she said. 'She won't have to be there long.

Being a month early, she doesn't have full strength, but apart from that she's doing well. Once she's through this she can have a wonderful life.'

He looked at the tiny creature who lay with her eyes closed, clearly unaware of the world she had entered.

'My little girl,' he whispered. 'Mine. And Ellie's.' He leaned closer. 'Your mother and I are going to be so happy with you. She'll be well soon, and she'll hold you in her arms.'

The doctor appeared in the doorway. 'Would you like to come back in now?' he asked.

'Is she—what's happening?'

'She's still losing blood. We're doing our best but it may not be enough.'

'Not enough?' he echoed wildly. 'She can't die—she mustn't—'

'We'll keep her alive if we can,' the doctor assured him.

'But *can* you?'

'I hope so, but I can't give you a promise just now. Please come in.'

He returned to the delivery room. Ellie lay there, still and quiet.

'Ellie,' he whispered. 'Ellie, can you hear me?'

'Yes—yes.'

She hardly made a sound, but the movement of her lips encouraged him.

'It's me, Leonizio. I'm here. I'll always be here

for you. And you must always be here for me. I
can't lose you. I couldn't bear it. Promise not to
leave me. Promise. Promise.'

At last she opened her eyes. He moved his face
closer, desperately seeking some sign that she understood him. But she looked at him in confusion.

'Promise me,' he repeated frantically. 'I
couldn't endure life without you. I love you.'

'Me?' she whispered. 'Love me?'

'Of course. You must always have known—'

'No—no—'

'But you know now. Tell me that you understand, please? *Please.*'

There was no response. Her eyes had closed
again and for a terrifying moment he thought the
worst had happened. But then he saw that she was
breathing. She was still alive, but she had slipped
away into another dimension and he must somehow find the strength to wait patiently for her to
return to him.

But perhaps she would never return. She was
close to death and he had a despairing feeling
that his pleas to her had gone unheard. Perhaps
for ever.

He leaned down so that his face was against
hers.

'Wherever you are,' he whispered, 'come back
to me. Please come back. *Please, Ellie, don't
leave me.*'

* * *

Ellie had the sensation of wandering through a corridor of shadows. She was in a place where she had never been before, not knowing what lay ahead, able only to hear mysterious voices. One of them sounded like Leonizio's.

'Ellie, can you hear me?'

She whispered, 'Yes,' but she couldn't be really sure what she heard. Leonizio's voice was speaking of love, saying he couldn't live without her.

She opened her eyes, hoping that he was there, but she could see nothing clearly.

'I couldn't endure life without you. I love you.'

'Me?' she whispered in disbelief. 'Love me?'

He spoke again but she couldn't make out the words. She knew now that it was a delusion. She believed in his love because she longed for it, but the mists were swirling her away and unconsciousness was claiming her again.

Now only one sound reached her. A desperate voice, whispering—

Wherever you are, come back to me. Please come back. *Ellie, come back!*

She turned, reaching out with her hands and her heart. But there was only the mist swirling about her until everything else vanished.

She didn't know how long she was unconscious, but when she awoke her mind was clear.

'Ah, good, you're back with us,' said the nurse.

'My baby—?'

'She's fine. A little small but she looks good.'

'She?'

'Yes, you've got a lovely little daughter. Her father's enchanted with her.'

'He's here?'

'He brought you into the hospital.'

'Oh, yes, I think I remember. But it's so confused. I can't be sure of anything.'

'He was with you during the birth. He left to spend a little time with your baby, but he came back a few minutes later. We were getting worried in case you didn't survive, and he just had to be with you. When we told him the danger was past he nearly collapsed. He's with your little girl now, telling her she's lucky to still have a *mamma*.'

'Oh—goodness!'

'Hey, don't cry. Everything's going to be all right.'

Everything all right, she thought wistfully as memories of her dream haunted her.

It had been an impossible fantasy, with Leonizio reaching out to her, declaring love in words she could never hope to hear in real life.

She was vaguely aware that the nurse had gone away, but she wasn't alone. She thought Leonizio stood there, watching her with anxious eyes. She held her breath, fearful that this too was a fantasy.

He came to sit by the bed, leaning close enough to talk softly.

'Thank you,' he said. 'Thank you for coming back to me. I dared to hope you couldn't leave me after I begged you to stay.'

'You—begged me—?'

'Don't you remember?'

'I'm not sure. Did we—talk?'

'Ellie, what do you mean? How can you ask if we talked? We said things we've never said before, perhaps because the moment was never right before. I told you that I loved you. You didn't seem to believe me, but it's the truth. Don't you remember?'

'I was in a strange place. I was walking through a dark mist and heard your voice, calling me.'

He hesitated, then asked quietly, 'Did you know the place you were heading for?'

'No, but I think now—that if you hadn't made me come back—' she trembled '—I would never have returned.'

'That's what I was afraid of,' he said. 'You were so close to—' He paused, unwilling to say the word. 'I couldn't have endured it. How could you go away from me when I love you so?'

'Do you really—love me? Truly?'

'Why can't you believe me? Haven't I begged you to marry me all this time?'

'Only because of the baby. You wanted to love someone who would always be there for you, a child who would return your love because it was yours. After what Harriet did, you needed your own child even more. And I could give you one. That was all I meant to you. I was sure of it.'

'Perhaps that was true once, but the longer we were together the more you came to mean to me. And that scared me.'

'Scared? You?'

'It takes a lot to scare me, but you managed it as nothing else ever could. I think my love for you began our first night together, when I discovered your warmth and kindness, and I was so glad to fall into your arms. It was a sweet feeling but it took me time to realise how it had taken me over. And then I was horrified to realise the love was all on my side.'

'But it wasn't. It isn't. I do love you. I've loved you for a long time.'

'How can you say that when you've always refused to marry me?'

'Because I couldn't bear the thought of an unequal marriage, loving you but knowing that you didn't love me.'

'I did love you, all the time. When you refused to marry me it hurt, and not just because of the baby. I wanted you. Nobody but you. But I thought you despised me, and I must work hard to overcome your scorn.'

'How strange that you should say that,' she murmured.

'Why?'

'Because sometimes I've felt that it was you who felt scorn for me.'

'Ellie, no, you can't have felt that.'

'I've longed for some sign that you cared for me, not just the baby. It never came. You minded about the baby, but never me.'

'That's not how it was. I minded about you so much I was afraid to face it. But even then—I knew I loved you, but until today I didn't fully understand how deep my love is. When I thought you were dying I couldn't bear to think of what my life would be without you. A blank desert with no hope of any kind.'

'But if that had happened—if I wasn't with you any more—you'd still have our child.'

'And I'd treasure her, for her own sake and in memory of you. I'd have called her Ellie, after you, because I can't survive without an Ellie in my life. Now I'd like to call her Cosima. It means order and beauty, which is what you both mean to me.

'You must promise to stay with me. Nothing and nobody could ever console me for losing you.

Please, Ellie, tell me that I can hope. I'll do all I can to win your love, however long it takes.'

'But I've already told you that I love you. Don't you believe me?'

'I'm almost afraid to. If you believe in good news too easily, it can get snatched away. You warned me of that once yourself.'

'It won't be snatched away, I promise you, Leonizio. You are my love, now and for ever.'

'Do you love me enough to marry me?'

'I always have.'

'Say yes,' he begged. 'Just that one word. Let me hear it.'

'Yes. Yes, I'll marry you. Yes.'

For a moment he didn't move. His eyes met hers, full of happiness and adoration. Then he lowered his head, resting it against her breast like a man who'd finally found the way home to a safe haven. It was a feeling that Ellie completely understood because it was her own.

'Yes,' she repeated. 'We took too long to find each other, but now we have and nothing will separate us. We're together—all three of us.'

'All three of us,' he repeated. 'Marry me, and I ask for nothing else.'

He glanced up as the doctor appeared.

'We're going to be married as soon as she's out of here,' he said. 'When will that be?'

'I'm afraid I can't tell you,' the doctor said uneasily. 'The danger isn't over yet.'

'But we thought—when she came round—'

'That was hopeful, but not final.'

'You mean she might still die?' Leonizio was aghast.

'I'm afraid it's possible.'

Leonizio dropped his head, putting a hand over his eyes. Ellie reached out to touch his face.

'Then we must marry now,' she whispered.

'Ellie—'

'If I'm going to die,' she said urgently, 'I want to die as your wife.'

He dropped to his knees beside the bed and she felt his tears against her skin.

She looked up at the doctor. 'Will you arrange it?'

'Yes,' he said, and hurried away.

Ellie stroked Leonizio's face, saying softly, 'If I do die, it's better for you if we're married. You'll find it easier to claim our baby.'

'That's not why I'm marrying you,' he said fiercely. 'I want you. No one but *you*.'

'I'll be there. Even if I'm not alive—I'll always be there with you.'

'And you will be alive. You simply must be because to lose you would break my heart for ever.'

'Together,' she whispered. 'Always together.'

The doctor appeared again.

'It has to be a civil ceremony,' he said. 'That's all we can arrange under these circumstances. Of course you can have a religious ceremony later.'

He didn't add, *if you're alive*, but they both understood.

'How quickly can we do this?' Ellie asked.

'Yes, we've waited too long,' Leonizio said, looking at her.

'I'm sorry,' she whispered. 'I should have understood before—'

'Don't blame yourself,' he said, leaning close. 'It's my fault that you didn't understand—I did everything wrong. But at last we've found the way and can marry now.'

'There are some formalities that have to be gone through first,' said the doctor. 'The law requires us to establish that the patient is in her right mind and acting of her own free will.'

'But I am,' Ellie said urgently. 'I'm doing what I want more than anything in the world. Please, please, sign anything you need, to confirm that.'

Fear was rising in her. Only a few minutes ago she had seemed to be slipping away into the darkness and Leonizio had drawn her back with his love. But, despite the power of her heart, her body was still weak and the darkness beckoned again.

For months she had loved him and longed to be his wife, despite the problems that made her refuse him. Now her moment had come, but perhaps it had come too late. In a few minutes they would have lost each other. When he raised his head and met her eyes she knew that he too understood everything.

The doctor returned with a middle-aged man that he introduced as Mr Dale, an official who could perform the ceremony.

'There are two kinds of vows,' he said. 'First, the traditional ones that everyone speaks. But then there are some more vows that you create for yourselves, that express your own true feelings. Do you think you can manage them?'

'Oh, yes,' Ellie said fervently.

Leonizio nodded. 'Yes,' he said softly.

Mr Dale handed them papers with the official vows, and looked around to check that the doctor and a nurse were present as witnesses. 'Now we can begin,' he said. He uttered the introductory words, then glanced at Leonizio, who took a deep breath as though trying to control his nerves, and began to speak.

'I, Leonizio, take you, Ellie, to be my wedded wife.'

Mr Dale nodded, then looked at Ellie.

She tightened her grasp on Leonizio's hand and said fervently, 'I, Ellie, take you, Leonizio, to be my wedded husband.'

Watching his face, she thought she saw the gleam of tears upon his cheeks, and felt her own tears begin to flow. To her horror, she could feel her strength fading and knew that they had only a little time left to belong to each other.

But she would make the most of that time, for Leonizio's sake. It was the only thing she could do for him before their terrible parting.

'What personal vows do you wish to make?' Mr Dale asked.

Gently Leonizio laid her hand against his lips.

'I promise that nobody in the world will ever matter more to me than you,' he said in a gentle voice. 'I belong to you now and for ever. You are my life, and that is what you will always be. Only promise me the same, and I will have all I'll ever want.'

There was an urgent question in his eyes, fixed on her, pleading.

'I can promise you the same,' she said. 'And I do. I am yours. I have been yours from the first moment, and I will always be yours.'

'Always?' he whispered.

'Always—and for ever.'

She saw joy come into his eyes as she said 'for ever' and hoped that he could see the same joy in her eyes as they committed themselves to each other.

At last came the declaration. *You are now man and wife.*

'We're married,' he whispered. 'You belong to me and I belong to you.'

'Yes. I'm going to stay with you always. Even if I should—'

'Don't say it,' he said urgently. 'That mustn't happen. You've got to live because I can't endure life without you.'

'Then I will,' she said.

'Swear it.'

'I swear by everything I hold sacred.'

She had given her word and she knew she must keep it at all costs. To lose her would devastate him in a way she had never imagined. Feeling sleep overtaking her, she struggled to fight it off.

Watching her, Leonizio was suddenly terrified. 'Ellie—Ellie—'

'It's all right,' the doctor said, feeling her pulse. 'She's stronger already.'

'Already? How can you tell so soon?'

'Because the tide has turned. Something—or someone—has given her the strength to fight for life much more strongly than before.'

Something or someone? Looking down at her in his arms, he wondered if their marriage could really have provided her with a reason for living. Was he hoping for too much?

As the minutes passed he felt the dawn of hope. Holding her in his arms, he murmured, 'Stay with me, Ellie. You promised—you promised—'

Gradually he sensed her breathing grow stronger until at last she opened her eyes again and he could see in them everything he longed for.

'You're better,' he breathed. 'You're going to live. Can't you feel that?'

She smiled. 'Of course I am. I promised. And I'll never break a promise to you for as long as I live.'

Now they were legally married, but when Ellie was released from hospital they both wanted another ceremony to proclaim their love to the world.

On their wedding morning he awoke to find her sitting on the bed beside him, with Cosima in her arms. The sight flooded him with peace and happiness, which was how it would always be, he realised.

They'd travelled to Rome for the ceremony. Many of Leonizio's employees were there, anxious not to miss the sight of the woman who had transformed their employer. Some of her friends, including Alex, came over from England.

When Ellie appeared in her bridal gown there was a murmur of astonishment, for she was carrying little Cosima in her arms. Leonizio's eyes were fixed on them with joy, and a whisper went around that he was marrying both of them.

Then it was time to answer questions. The

preacher asked, 'Do you take this woman to be your wedded wife?'

Leonizio's eyes met Ellie's. 'A thousand times over,' he said quietly.

The preacher looked uneasily at the bride. 'That's not the answer you're supposed to give.'

'Don't worry,' Ellie said. 'To me it's the perfect answer.'

A little gulp came from Cosima. Both her parents smiled at her in delight.

'We're agreed,' Leonizio said. 'All three of us.'

'Yes,' Ellie said. 'All three of us.'

And that, they both knew, was how it would always be.

* * * * *

Eva stared into his eyes, a million confusing truths racing
through her brain. This was the unspoken reality of what
happened to people with destinies. It was all there in his
eyes. People with destinies rarely got what they wanted.
Duty and responsibility came first.

Would she throw it all away for one night with a man
she longed for? The first man she'd ever really wanted?

She swallowed. She'd thought the answer would be
easy. Instead, she stood frozen. How could she decide
without a kiss? Without a touch?

Her lips tingled at the thought of another kiss. Her
entire body exploded at the thought of more of his touch.
Something must have changed in her expression because
he pulled back. "No. I can't be the person who steals your
destiny from you."

Her eyes clung to his. "There is one way."

His eyebrows rose.

"I know I told you I wouldn't force you to stay
married...but what if we wanted to?"

"Stay married?"

She nodded.

He squeezed his eyes shut. "You have known me four weeks. I can't ask for a life commitment after four weeks."

"But you were willing to marry a princess you didn't know."

"And now I know her and now I know she deserves more. Real love. Trust. A man who doesn't have walls."

He turned her in the direction of her room. "Go, before I can't be noble anymore."

Don't miss
WEDDED FOR HIS ROYAL DUTY
by Susan Meier,
available July 2016 wherever
Harlequin® Romance books and ebooks are sold.

www.Harlequin.com

HREXP0616

Reading Has Its Rewards

Earn **FREE BOOKS!**

Register at **Harlequin My Rewards** and submit your Harlequin purchases from wherever you shop to earn points for free books and other exclusive rewards.

Plus submit your purchases from now till May 30th for a chance to win a $500 Visa Card*.

Visit **HarlequinMyRewards.com** today

Earn **FREE** REWARDS
Join Today!
HarlequinMyRewards.com

MYR16R1